HOW TO BE SAFE

ALSO BY TOM McALLISTER

The Young Widower's Handbook

Bury Me in My Jersey

HOW TO
BE SAFE

A NOVEL

TOM McALLISTER

LIVERIGHT PUBLISHING CORPORATION

A Division of W. W. Norton & Company

Independent Publishers Since 1923

New York • London

How to Be Safe is a work of fiction. With the obvious exception of certain well-known historical and public figures, all characters (and the situations, incidents, and dialogue concerning them) are products of the author's imagination. In all other respects, any resemblance to persons living or dead is entirely coincidental.

For information about permission to reproduce selections from this book, write to Permissions, Liveright Publishing Corporation, a division of W. W. Norton & Company, Inc., 500 Fifth Avenue, New York, NY 10110

For information about special discounts for bulk purchases, please contact W. W. Norton Special Sales at specialsales@wwnorton.com or 800-233-4830

Manufacturing by Quad Graphics Fairfield
Book design by Dana Sloan
Production manager: Lauren Abbate

Library of Congress Cataloging-in-Publication Data

Names: McAllister, Tom, author.
Title: How to be safe : a novel / Tom McAllister.
Description: First edition. | New York : Liveright Publishing Corporation, a division of W. W. Norton & Company, [2018]
Identifiers: LCCN 2017054671 | ISBN 9781631494130 (hardcover)
Subjects: LCSH: Life change events—Fiction. | Women teachers—Fiction. | City and town life—Fiction. | GSAFD: Black humor (Literature) | Satire.
Classification: LCC PS3613.C2653 H69 2018 | DDC 813/.6—dc23
LC record available at https://lccn.loc.gov/2017054671

Liveright Publishing Corporation, 500 Fifth Avenue, New York, N. Y. 10110
www.wwnorton.com

W. W. Norton & Company Ltd., 15 Carlisle Street, London W1D 3BS

1 2 3 4 5 6 7 8 9 0

For my parents—Mom, Dad, and Fred

PROLOGUE

WITH SOME TIME to kill, the shooter parks his car outside One Brother's Pizza and he thinks: It's just a slice, a slice won't slow me down. He thinks: A slice may even be good for me. He thinks: This is a choice, I'm making a choice and nobody in the world has any say over whether or not I make this choice.

Last night, he forgot to eat. Even after a full month of planning, there were loose ends to tie up, there were final considerations. He hadn't wanted to leave a note, but while he lay in bed not sleeping there were so many words in his mind desperate to escape and he could feel them crawling like cockroaches out of his mouth and so he decided to record them in his notebook. Later they will find his notebook and call it a manifesto. The media will try to analyze it and explain it, but they are dull and they cannot be trusted to understand.

Next door to One Brother's is a small insurance agency with an oversized window, in which a pretty middle-aged woman sits as if on display. Her desk faces away from the street, but her body is turned so that he can see her profile, the cold curve of her cheekbone, the skin beneath her jaw sagging like an ill-fitting mask. He stands only three feet away from her, separated by the glass like a prisoner at visitation. Her blond hair is cut in a bob and swept stylishly across her forehead, and she wears a blouse and skirt like something a mannequin at a high-end department store would wear. Her legs crossed with her cell phone resting in the valley between her thighs, she stares down intently at her crotch, occasionally laughing and swiping fingers across the screen. She looks like a well-adjusted version of his mother. Like his mother if she'd had better parents and gone to a good high school and been able to earn an associate's degree in something. If she would just look up from her phone she would see him and they could make eye contact and have something like a human connection, they could hold hands and have a picnic and dance in a field to a Billy Joel song and smoke cigarettes together under the moon, but she is playing a game with bright colors and cute cartoon birds, and in those brief moments when she looks away from the screen she seems to be thinking about something unpleasant, a fight with her ex-husband or her son's college applications, or maybe trying to convince herself that the weird mole on her neck is nothing and she's going to be fine.

The phone on her desk rings and she pivots to answer it, turning her back to him.

She will see him on the news later and not even know how close he'd been to her, how she could have saved everyone if only she'd taken the time.

Across the street, there is a gas station flanked by a ten-foot-tall brontosaurus statue, the dinosaur smiling grimly as if he's just become aware of the extinction of his species, of the incurable loneliness that will plague him until he dies. It's a pretty dark joke by the proprietors, he thinks, a reminder that the fuel pumping into patrons' cars is the liquefied remains of millennia of once-living things, some long extinct. Every car is full of dead things, churning and grinding and conveying people from one place to another and eventually the people are dead too and replaced by other people. The monetization of large-scale death, the repurposing of extinction.

He enters One Brother's, where the pizza is laid out like jewelry in a glass case. He points at a slice with pepperoni and the man behind the counter slides the slice into the oven to heat it up, then turns his attention back to the TV in the corner of the room, which is tuned to a talk show that must be made for children and adults who have suffered traumatic brain injuries. The panel of hosts is debating the proper etiquette for farting in a restaurant; the audience laughs like a roomful of dope fiends who have just gotten their fix.

It is eleven o'clock. By noon, he will have killed nineteen people, wounded forty-five. He is armed extensively, enough to take out more than that, but his gun will jam and one of his homemade bombs will not detonate.

The pizza scalds the roof of his mouth and he feels the skin peeling off with the bubbling cheese and he drops the slice back onto the plate, sauce slopping out of his burning mouth and searing his chin and he thinks: Fucking pizza pizza fucking fuck all the fucks. Then he thinks: I could just do it here. Then he thinks: If that guy looks at me again. Then he thinks: Play it cool. You made a plan for a reason.

Later, the pundits will speculate. They will look for reasons. They will want to know why. They will call him a loner and they will quote former teachers saying he was bright but shy and they never thought he'd be capable of something like this. They will say, *Nobody ever suspected it could happen here.*

The pepperoni is unctuous and too round too obviously manufactured too hot too crispy too indifferent. Pepperoni is made from dead animals, he reminds himself. They died for you. Like Christ except at least pepperoni serves a function. There are two jobs in the slaughterhouse, the slaughtered and the slaughterer. Most of them don't even know until it's too late.

There will be a hero teacher who tackles him, and that hero teacher will be the last one to die.

He bites into the pizza again and now it's not too hot, it's so-called just right and as he grinds it with his teeth and feels it sliding down his throat, it goes to that place in him that craves garbage, that is insatiable in its pursuit of grease and sugar and fat, that place in him he would cut out if he could because then someone else could be the fat kid at school, the slob, the punch line. He feels the grease cooling inside him, congealing, and he feels at the same time satisfied and helpless and angry, and then he takes another bite.

Everyone eats a last meal, even if most don't realize it at the time. You have a bowl of grain-based flakes and skim milk before heading to work and having a stroke at your desk. His father's last meal was a hot roast beef sandwich and a bag of chips, washed down with between eight and twelve beers. He didn't come home from the bar, but that wasn't unusual; they didn't even think anything was wrong until the police called and said they'd found his car and someone ought to come in and identify the body.

Rasputin's last meal was sturgeon in Champagne sauce and poisoned honeyed cakes. Eichmann had half a bottle of red wine. Timothy McVeigh had two pints of mint chocolate-chip ice cream. John Wayne Gacy ate deep-fried shrimp with fried chicken and strawberries.

Gerald Lee Mitchell—a bag of Jolly Ranchers. Patrick Rogers—a single glass of Coke. Stacey Lawton—a jar of pickles. James Edward Smith—a clump of dirt. Dozens of condemned men ate pizza before they faced the firing squad or the chair or the injection. Everyone in the pizza shop is condemned, he thinks, they just don't have the luxury of knowing how or when the end is going to come.

The door behind him swings open, bells ringing, a cop jangling fat and sloppy to the counter, too dumb to know what's going to happen. Too dumb to even suspect. He is jovial and everyone here knows him. He carries himself like the world is a good and fine place and like there is meaning in being an overweight small-town policeman who spends his days in a pizza parlor watching terrible TV.

The officer will be one of dozens pursuing the shooter through the woods near the school, and he will be maimed by one of the traps laid there in advance. He will lose his left hand and sustain severe burns on the left side of his face and he will never work active duty again. After nine months of rehab he will try to reclaim his life but will never again feel like the world is a good or fine place.

The shooter is finished, except for the crust—eating the crust is unnatural, it's like eating the bones—and he wants to make a grand gesture when he leaves, give everyone in that room a story, so that years from now they can tell people that the day the shooting happened, they saw him. So they can say: *I can't believe it could have been me.* So they can say: *I could tell something wasn't right with that kid, but I didn't think he'd do that.* So they can say: *If I could just go back and do it over again I would have stopped him.* But you can't do things over again. That's the point. He wants them to understand the randomness of fate, to understand that he himself is fate personified, and he chose not to kill them, not because they're special or more important or better prepared or more faithful or more likable, but because there is no reason but unreason. He rises and goose-steps toward the exit, his heavy boots pounding a warning into the floor. At the door, he pivots on his heels and salutes the room. He holds this pose for a moment, whistling "Taps," and then lowers his hand deliberately, like the soldier standing before him and his mother at his father's funeral. He turns sharply on his heels and leaves the pizza shop.

He will not survive the shooting. Has no intention of surviving the shooting. There is no escape; anywhere he goes will be the same. He will run only so that they chase him.

His mother, drunk and alone at home, is watching TV and may not even know he has left the house. Next month, she will have a last meal of Canadian Club and onion rings and a hundred aspirin. Her boyfriend, Don, will be investigated for murder when they find the bruises on her arms, but he will have an airtight alibi. He will try to wring the most out of the low-level celebrity he gains from his association with the whole ugly mess, but in the end he will still be the same sad man he always was. In seventeen years Don will have a final meal of three saltines and some broth spoon-fed to him by the hospice nurse.

He pulls into the school parking lot. It is fourth period. Soon hundreds of his classmates will be herded into the cafeteria and they will fill themselves with fried food and they will be *so loud*. They think they have unlimited time and they think the things they care about matter but those things do not matter. The first shots will be fired in the cafeteria during lunchtime, and there will be explosives planted at the doors so anyone trying to escape will be exploded. He will stalk the halls, firing randomly through barricaded doors and catching the stragglers who are stuck without a hiding place. He will pull the fire alarm to make them think he set fire to the building and he will pick them off as they flee. The hero teacher will be shot through the lungs because this is not a world for heroes. This is a world for villains, this is a world for grand statements, not subtlety.

After the shooting, they will investigate his journals and his music and his web browsing history and they will try to paint a portrait that makes sense; they will shape a narrative around him that suggests the possibility of solutions. During the autopsy, they will find the pizza in his stomach, and they will find the residue of Adderall and Ritalin in his blood, and they will cut his brain open hoping to find some clue about what makes

7

people like him exist, but they will find nothing besides what they always find. His brain is just another brain. It's connected to someone with a bad soul, but you can't bottle that or study it. The slivers of his brain placed on slides under a microscope will not show the memories, won't allow them to read the rejection and the emptiness and the abuse and the fear. The slides will not show the ways people can be ruined just by existing in the world. Shell-shocked acquaintances will say without irony that he had so much to live for, ignorant of the fact that the prospect of having to live like this for another fifty years was not the solution to but rather the cause of his hopelessness.

He leaves his car running and doesn't bother closing the door. The walk to the school is short, only a few hundred feet, and he feels himself gliding across that distance. He feels suddenly deprived of his senses, blind and deaf and numb. There is no heaven and there is no hell and there is no afterlife there is only now. There will be no white light for him to walk toward. He himself is the light toward which others will walk. He enters the school and then feels his material form disintegrating in the heat as he turns into a red giant star and then goes supernova and collapses on himself and becomes a neutron star, impossibly dense and powerful, and everyone nearby is drawn toward him by the immense gravitational force and then he's a black hole and then he is nothing at all just cosmic dust that used to be something.

APRIL

AFTER, THE SUN turned gray and descended into the lake like a spider dropping from the ceiling. I saw it hit the water, I saw the steam rising up, and I felt the tremors when it crashed against the lake floor. I saw the displaced water splashing over the banks and rushing toward our houses.

The experts say the sun is too big to fit into the lake, that it can't just fall, but they can't explain the darkness, or the fog that hovered over us for weeks. They say it's basic science—a falling sun would extinguish the world—but I know what I saw. I trust the things I see. I spent much of my life trying to believe in things I'd read. I went through school. I'm educated. I know all the things I'm supposed to believe. But in what world do any of them seem right? Every fact they try to sell you can be disproven if you look in the right places. Everyone says truth is an objective thing, but what if I find a different truth that makes more sense?

• • •

I heard the gunshots, but they didn't register as gunshots. I'd only heard a gun in real life twice before that day. The first time was when I was very young, when my father made me go on a hunting trip with him and his brother. It was an attempt to bond with an estranged sibling, to reconnect with some primitive vision of masculinity. He'd fired the gun in front of me, hoping to impress me, but all I remember is the look of monstrous glee on his face. The day of the shooting at the school, I thought at first that I'd just heard distant construction or a car accident. I was home when it happened. I hadn't been at work for two weeks, because I'd been told I was not wanted at work. They had suspended me for a so-called outburst.

Suspension of the right to work. That's what the official letter from the school district had said. Rights get suspended and pants get suspended and bridges get suspended. How does it all work? I don't know; I'm not an engineer. Everyone is suspended in some way, until they're not. The sun had been suspended in our sky for eons and then it had seen enough.

◆ ◆ ◆

I watched the news. I ignored my phone though it buzzed incessantly. My email inbox overflowed with people asking questions I could not answer. I deleted everything without reading it. My brother was trying to contact me but I was afraid to answer. What could I say to him under these circumstances? I was very bad at lying to my brother, and I didn't want to frighten him. On TV they called it a rampage, then they called it a massacre, then they called it a state of emergency, then they settled back on massacre.

. . .

I saw the faces. I saw Sara R with the blood on her blouse being led into the back of an ambulance. I saw Kelsey P in the grass where sometimes I would teach my English classes on nice days. I saw a circle of students holding hands in prayer. I saw the windows shattered and the fire smoldering in the gym. These were people I knew, lying dead in places I knew. Changing the channel did not make it disappear. Sometimes life is so graphic it's impossible to process.

On TV they speculated. Could it be terrorism? Maybe it was a student. Maybe it was a drill gone horribly wrong. A disgruntled former employee. A random act of violence. An escaped convict. An angel of death. A different kind of terrorist. To be on the news, you just need to own a suit and be willing to guess about anything. You become someone who opines for a living. Opinions need to happen fast, or they don't count.

They were grasping for suspects, and they showed pictures of recently fired employees. They showed my face. They said my name. This is Anna Crawford, they said. She was recently fired from her job as an English teacher for insubordination. She posted a message online saying she hates the place. She said, and I quote, I should've burned the place down when I had the chance. She added hashtag bitter hashtag spite hashtag fuck that place. On the screen, the text said: FORMER TEACHER HAD MOTIVE.

Until that report aired, I was unaware that I had been fired. I thought I was suspended.

The knocking started minutes later.

◆ ◆ ◆

It was the media first. They filmed me through the windows. And I remember thinking, beyond anything else: I am not wearing a bra. They are going to see that I'm not wearing a bra, and it is going to be on TV.

The news was running on a five-second delay, so as I watched the media assembling outside my house, I was also watching my recent past self on the screen. She looked so much younger than me. I felt a pang of nostalgia for the life I'd been living just minutes ago.

I felt the international media rustling through my pockets and ransacking my life, dumping out drawers, hoping to find evidence that I had committed a mass murder a mile away from my home. I felt their hands all over me, violating me. I opened my door and shouted: "You *do not* have permission. I don't grant it to you."

I shouldn't have opened the door. When the barbarians are at the gates, you do not lower the drawbridge, even if you have something really important to say. One of them entered my house, and there was a scuffle. The next thing I knew I was in the back of a police car, still being filmed. Later I would watch the video and see that I was laughing as they drove me away. I can't explain that. I don't remember it at all.

◆ ◆ ◆

While I was gone, the FBI destroyed my home. They broke holes in my drywall looking for caches of weapons. They tore up the carpets and poured my trash cans onto the floor. They found nothing incriminating. Later, they would leave a note saying, "The FBI was compelled by your behaviors to search your home. The FBI is not responsible for any damage incurred by your home during this search. By reading this document, you agree to the terms above." They say the FBI doesn't have a sense of humor, but they're wrong. The FBI loves to laugh.

◆ ◆ ◆

Nobody told me what was happening. On TV, they reported that I was a person of interest, not under arrest. They were just interested in me, which allowed them to deny my rights.

After five hours, they gave me some water. They told me that when they came back I'd better be ready to tell them everything. They didn't come back for another five hours.

◆ ◆ ◆

During the few days they held me prisoner, my entire life had been shared with the world.

I had become public property.

Everyone knew by then who the shooter was, but there was a frantic hunt for possible co-conspirators. On the Internet, they pored over all the scraps of my life they could find.

Hundreds of websites posted articles investigating inconsistencies in my alibi. My biography had become so-called content, a disposable distraction to keep people occupied for a week. Someone with thousands of followers posted my home address. High school classmates suddenly had stories about me they needed to tell. They remembered me being weird. "She always kind of creeped me out," a person named Corey said. I don't remember ever meeting anyone named Corey. I wasn't even sure Corey could be a person's name. Reports cited anonymous sources talking about everything I'd ever done wrong— shoplifting, taking too many smoke breaks at work, knocking over a neighbor's mailbox after an argument. An ex shared nude photos of me, because, he said, anyone who could kill kids had lost her right to privacy. Later, a reporter asked me if I was embarrassed by the pictures, if I wanted to apologize for taking them.

◆ ◆ ◆

They found my brother, Calvin, while I was in jail. Not that he was hiding from them. He'd moved away years ago so he could be free of this town and all the people in it. I didn't see the video until later. He stood in his doorway holding his toddler daughter, who buried her head in his chest to hide from the camera's lights. I hadn't seen his face in a very long time; he still sent me videos and pictures, but he was always behind the camera, recording his children and his wife. His hair was receding prematurely, and he looked like he'd lost weight. Like he'd been working out. He listened politely to the reporter's question, and he said, "What exactly do you want from me?" He stepped closer to the camera. "What do you want me to say to you?"

The reporter stood his ground and said, "We'd like you to share your thoughts on your sister's alleged involvement in the Seldom Falls Massacre."

Calvin glared at him and I saw his eyes flash with the old menace. I saw him trying to decide whether it was worth it to assault the reporter. "Motherfucker, I don't share my thoughts," he said, and went back in his house.

◆ ◆ ◆

In the days after the shooting, the news anchors all thought they were being very clever by pointing out that it had occurred in what was once America's friendliest city. A major magazine had given this honor to Seldom Falls, PA, three times in the '80s, when I was still young enough to believe in such things. Many of the shops on Main Street have faded signs in their windows saying WELCOME TO AMERICA'S FRIENDLIEST CITY. It's not even technically a city anymore, not since the population was cut in half. It's a township. The friendliness is a commodity in a town with nothing else to sell. When people come here, it's because they're on the way to somewhere else, or because they want to be left alone. They rent a cabin near the lake and spend a week hiding from whatever they left behind. It was easy to fill in the blanks on the template: idyllic small town, never thought it would happen here, shocked residents, B-roll of trees and nature. Our proximity to nature was supposed to inoculate us against the evils of the big city, but nature is crueler than anything man can invent. Nature kills for no reason every day. If you want to make people safe, the best thing to do is to ban nature, to arrest nature and put it in jail where it can't bother us anymore.

◆ ◆ ◆

In the late eighteenth century, a pair of brothers named Seth and Ephraim Seldom settled here among the natives and declared themselves the owners of this land. They'd been born to an aristocratic family in Rhode Island, but had to flee due to a conflict with the local church. There are no falls here, but the gusting of the wind over the lake can rustle the trees loudly enough that it sounds like a distant waterfall. A number of streets are now named after the natives who lived here, a lukewarm penance for colonizing their land. We didn't learn much about what happened to the natives, but I know their blood saturates the soil. I can taste the blood in the crops the farmers grow here. When I was twelve, I spent a week during my summer vacation digging a hole in the backyard so I could hide in it during the day; each time I cut into the earth, I knew I was slicing through the degraded bodies of natives, knew each rock could be the fossilized bones of massacred people.

◆ ◆ ◆

The school was a safe school. It was in a safe town. It was attended by safe people. Everyone kept repeating these lies. We are not like those other schools, they said. At my first teaching job after college, in the kind of unsafe place where they send inexperienced teachers, we had daily briefings running down the previous day's fights. We were required to take self-defense classes. That school was the first one in the city to install metal detectors and put bars over the windows. When I told people where I worked, they gasped as if I'd just told them I had cancer. Many of the families in Seldom Falls had fled here from nearby cities. My mother's father was mugged by a black man in Pittsburgh and three weeks later he moved here to start over. My father's father didn't like how many black families were moving into his neighborhood in Cleveland, so he left before his children could be degraded by the new neighbors. We were raised to understand that being here was what kept us safe. When I was young and our neighbors sold their house, they knocked on the door to assure my father they wouldn't sell to *the wrong kind of people*. The first time I ate a meal with a black person was in college, when I had lunch with classmates to discuss a group project. It was the first time in my entire life that I'd thought about what it meant to be white. Four years later, I was teaching at an urban school with only a handful of white students. We spent every day bracing for a violent eruption, but it was never as bad as they said it would be. Teenagers got in fights because they were teenagers. The boys lost their tempers and feuded over girls and hurt each other for sport. The girls stole from one another and got into screaming matches and every now and then one of them burst open with an intensity that could only be fueled by trauma. But the violence was all localized and contained. After a few years, I moved back here like everyone else thinking I could get away from the threat of violence, but violence goes wherever it wants. It's like water flowing through every crevice and breaking down your walls and dragging you screaming out to the sea.

MAY

THE POLICE DIDN'T drive me home when they were done with me. They just told me to go. This town is too small to have cabs and the buses are unreliable, so I walked a half mile to Renee's house.

Renee and I went to college together for a year, before she transferred out of state. I stopped taking classes six months later and moved to an apartment two blocks from where I grew up. I had no interest in going back to my parents' house, but some ineffable force kept me in its orbit. I was too immature then for college. I got a job as a waitress and spent nights trying to wash the smell of fried food out of my hair. I left my lights on all day and never closed my windows because I knew this would annoy my mother when she drove by and saw that I was being wasteful. My father knocked on my door once and asked if he could watch my TV because my mother had broken his. Otherwise, they never visited me.

Every time Renee came home, she told me how great the

parties were at her school, how lame Seldom Falls was, how, no matter what it took, I had to get away from this place. She moved back five years later with the man she would soon marry and eventually divorce. She'd had a miscarriage and then couldn't get pregnant again and he wanted children more than he wanted her. Now she owns a three-bedroom house that's too big.

I knocked on her door, and she pulled me inside and held me. She absorbed my tears until my head felt completely empty. I lay on her couch while she made tea. She forced me to eat something even though I'd lost my appetite so long ago I didn't remember ever liking food. I told her I heard the police helicopters in my dreams. I told her about the gunshots. She told me the media had been relentless in pressuring her for gossip, but she hadn't cracked.

Later, I would learn this wasn't true. Anybody who has information about you will give it up eventually, for the right price. For Renee, it was five hundred dollars and a new transmission for her Toyota. That was all it took for her give them pictures from my college years: me with the man I almost married, me flashing my middle finger at the camera, me doing shots in a bar. She was the *anonymous source close to the suspect* who said, "Anna means well, but she can be unstable. She's like an old cat, you know, how sometimes they love you and other times they want to claw your eyes out."

• • •

I had been publicly cleared of all wrongdoing, but that didn't matter. Conspiracy theorists thought I had probably done it and was being protected by the government for some reason. I received occasional emails from amateur detectives who accused me of helping the government run a false-flag operation. Others admitted I hadn't done the shooting—they acted like this was a gracious concession, admitting that all the facts existed as facts—but they still were convinced I was guilty of something. They needed me to be bad. Everything that happens is covering up some other thing that's even worse. Facts are not facts at all; they're just the first line of an argument.

By the time I returned to my house, the media had moved on from me. My lawn had been trampled and someone had pawed through my garbage. The inside had been ransacked by the FBI. I stepped over the wreckage and sorted through the pile of mail that had accumulated under the slot. There were two letters from Calvin. He'd gotten in the habit of writing letters when he was in rehab and wasn't allowed access to his phone or the Internet. The only people left in the country who write letters are prisoners. He had called a dozen times and sent me messages every day. I knew I had to call him back. I knew it wasn't fair to be silent. I had been hoping if I just pretended none of this was happening, I could save him from it.

I decided that if he called me again I would answer. It was his responsibility to try one more time, I thought. He called an hour after I walked through the front door.

"It's a good thing you answered," he said. "If you didn't, I was gonna drive over there and wait for you."

If I'd had to see him at that moment, I would have shattered. Sometimes you can love someone enough that you never want to see them. The love is too intense for you to be in the same room. Love is not magnetic, it is repulsive; it creates an energy of sickness and anxiety that can destroy everything. The Earth loves the sun, but it maintains a safe distance so it doesn't get incinerated.

"Just so you know," I said, "I didn't do the shooting."

"I know," he said.

"But you believed them when they said it."

"Honestly, if I knew it was an option when I was seventeen, I probably would have done it myself," he said.

• • •

The last time I had seen Calvin in Seldom Falls was at my mother's funeral. He hugged me and told me he loved me, and I told him again how sorry I was for not being better. He kneeled at the casket and prayed, and I did not know what he could be praying about, or to whom. I resented him for having the recourse of prayer, when I couldn't find a way to make it work for me. It felt like a betrayal for him to find solace in a god I couldn't identify. Did he love my mother? Did he love a god or Jesus or someone else?

I was never supposed to know I had a brother. My father thought he'd be able to keep it a secret, but he was not that clever a man. My parents were going through what my mother called "a rough patch." It was rough in the sense that they were realizing they'd made a terrible mistake by getting married. My father had married a twenty-two-year-old and resented her for aging. I could never picture him as a young man; he was always tired and old and hard. I could visualize my mother as a young woman, and every now and then imagined her as the sort of person I could have been friends with. Not good friends, but good enough. I was seven when my younger brother was born. My father had gotten a seventeen-year-old pregnant. She was a friend's daughter; they'd had an affair for several months. She wanted an abortion, but he wouldn't allow it, due to some latent religious convictions I'd never known he had. A year later, I learned about all of it while I ate breakfast before school. My father dunked a plain bagel in his tea and scanned the comics page. He dunked and dunked and then ate the soggy bagel. My mother glared at him across the table while I slurped on cereal. He didn't have a job then. He was planning on going out and applying, soon. Before I got up, my mother said, "So when does Anna get to meet her little brother?" I think my mother had waited that full year for him to finally come clean, getting angrier every day he acted as if nothing had happened. He dunked his bagel again, and then folded the paper calmly. "What an interesting question," he said, turning to me. "Isn't your mother just a fascinating woman?"

• • •

I had three fathers. There was the father I had as a child, the one I had after Calvin's existence was revealed, and the one I had after Calvin moved in with us, five years later. You don't have to explain the trinity to me, because I get it. There is the Loving Father, the Desperate Father, and the Defeated Father, and they are all one. It took me many years to understand all of this. The Loving Father left after his son was born. I didn't think this was my fault, but people kept telling me it was not my fault, and that made me certain it actually was my fault. The Desperate Father wanted to be something he could not be, something he had once been but had lost. The Loving Father had naturally bonded with me from the start and had been my best friend. Then, in that five-year gap between Calvin's birth and his move into our house, the Desperate Father tried too hard to prove he was still the man he used to be. He took me to sporting events and carnivals and concerts for nostalgia acts. He pulled me out of school during the day and took me to the movies. He hid gifts in my room, sneaking candy to me when my mother was asleep. He smiled too hard at me and he sweated constantly. He wanted something I could not give him, which was forgiveness for being a bad husband.

The Defeated Father either loved Calvin too much or not at all, and could not bear to look at him. He was living a life he didn't want anymore, and every time he looked at us, he was reminded of all the other lives he could have had. His silences were violent and I felt them from blocks away. Alone all night, he sat in the living room with the TV on mute and music playing in his ears.

• • •

It was clear the shooter had acted alone and that there were no co-conspirators, so now there was a rush to assign blame. Carl S, the guidance counselor, had to explain how he'd missed the red flags. The police had to explain how they'd missed the red flags. The shooter's few friends had to explain how they'd missed the red flags. There were red flags, the papers said. It's just that nobody saw them. When everything you see is a red flag, it's impossible to know which ones matter. If you are in danger everywhere you go, then you start to ignore all the warning signs.

The police were not equipped to handle a crime of this magnitude. Journalists found consistent breakdowns in the system. There had been a couple reports from the parents of a classmate who said the boy was acting strangely and lashing out over petty slights. He had posted bizarre things online, about hatred and vengeance and guns. But we lived in a town where people hunted, so everybody always bragged about their guns. Guns were gifts you got for thirteen-year-old boys. On Independence Day, the annual parade ended with shooting competitions, divided into senior, adult, and youth divisions. Before I was born, a teenager from Seldom Falls had placed fifth in the Olympics in the 300-meter rifle event.

But it was more than the guns. The shooter had written the word *"muerte"* in marker on the locker of the class president. A girl at school had accused him of snipping off chunks of her hair during class and keeping them in a Ziploc bag in his locker, but the principal had told them to settle it between themselves. The day of the shooting, the police rolled out their full arsenal but they had never practiced anything like an active shooter drill. On TV they said a faster response could have saved up to ten lives. Every parent or spouse of every victim had done the math and was convinced their son or daughter or husband or wife would have been among the up to ten spared. The chief of police had vowed not to resign in the face of public pressure. The mayor promised to double the security budget. He vowed to spare no expense. He said, "We are going to pursue safety obsessively and intensely. We will not be defeated."

· · ·

The mayor's name was Randy C. He was my age, but his hands were tiny and delicate and his face still looked like it did when we were in school together. If not for his receding hairline, he would have looked like a teen in a discount suit. He used to cheat off me in algebra, and once when we were both at a classmate's fourteenth birthday party, he and I ended up in a closet together for seven minutes. The popular kids drew our names from a hat then locked us in a closet and told us we were going to heaven. He'd never kissed anybody before and his tongue swirled around in my mouth like a dog trying to lick the last remnants of peanut butter out of the jar. He kept pressing his hands against the hook on my bra, but didn't have the courage to unclasp it. For the next two years he avoided eye contact with me. When we graduated from high school, he shook my hand and wished me a good life. "You be good, kid," he'd said.

· · ·

After you're killed, the media needs to determine whether you deserved to die. They need to know whether to feel sad for you. There is a finite amount of sadness in the world, and the only way to process a mass killing is if it turns out some of the victims were less deserving of life than others. They suggested that Abdul F, the graduate student who was shadowing teachers in the math department, had "self-radicalized" and that he could have become a threat to national security. They found that Joe M owed months of back child support. Ronnie B was a beloved physics teacher, but she also had written some strange antigovernment posts on social media and there had been rumors of a relationship with the principal, Hank T, who had a reputation for cheating on his wife. One by one they were tried and judged as slightly less worthy than the others. It was important for people to feel like the murders could somehow be justified.

They couldn't figure out how to feel better about the twelve dead children.

• • •

When my parents were young, they had newspapers and radio and TV, but there were limits on when and how they could access them. It was possible to develop a cohesive worldview and also to detach yourself from all of it when necessary. Now at all hours, I could watch the conservative news network or the liberal news network or the centrist news network. They all told me we were doomed, but for different reasons. The news networks were run by billionaires, and the on-air talent were wealthy New Yorkers who ate at the same restaurants and pledged allegiance to their ratings. They looked the same and they represented no meaningful ideology. They aided and abetted the shooters by confusing the narrative. They didn't know anything about the world but we trusted them because they dressed nicely and spoke with such certainty. I didn't know what I wanted from the news, but I kept returning and hoping for something better to happen, or at least to be able to witness the next awful thing. Every story was followed by a counterstory calling the original a lie, and then the journalists spent the day bickering about which stories were fake and which were not. It was impossible to believe anything, besides that we were in danger. You can consume so much media that it becomes toxic. The only option is to flush the system, to purge yourself and feel it burning in your esophagus then see it pooled at your feet.

• • •

The media found heroes, too. There was John K, the biology teacher who'd done a stint in the National Guard and led a weekly Bible discussion group after classes. He hustled the students into the gym and barricaded the door before chasing the shooter and trying to subdue him. The media kept coming back to his story as proof that good exists in the world. There was a redemptive arc. They showed photos of him with his own children and him in his uniform and him in church.

A syndicated columnist wrote that the cultural construct of masculinity was to blame. She wrote that there is a mass pathology afflicting men in this country, and the real solution is not to persecute an overworked guidance counselor, but instead to reshape societal values in such a way that boys aren't praised for violence and celebrated for suppressing their emotions. She said we're training them to be little killers with rage problems. The columnist received death threats online. In the comments they called her a bitch and said maybe she just needed to get fucked. They told her they wanted to kill her and fuck her, in that order.

• • •

Men think their dicks are the solution to every problem they face. When I was fourteen, my uncle asked me a question about school and I said something sarcastic back to him and everyone laughed, so later he grabbed my arm and pulled me aside and said, "Your tits aren't big enough to act like such a bitch." He squeezed my bicep and stared hard enough to let me know how easily he could break me. "What you need is to go and get fucked, and maybe you'll finally loosen up." I spent most of my time at future family events trying not to be alone in a room with him. I never told my parents. I was afraid they would blame me for it. I was even more afraid they would make me talk to my uncle about it. He never said anything like that again, but he didn't need to.

My problem is not a lack of dicks. My problem is an abundance of dicks, being surrounded by dicks, always being reminded that they're ready to be unsheathed and used as a corrective if I step out of line.

• • •

On TV, they told us it was not the right time to politicize the tragedy. You can't talk about it in the aftermath because nobody will listen. You can't talk about it later because then it's old news. It's in bad taste to use the victims to score political points. There is no right time to talk about the causes, because the event has already occurred and if you spend time talking about the causes then you're disrespecting the effects.

The news replayed the security footage endlessly. For a month, turning on the TV meant you might see grainy images of the shooter hustling up the stairs to the third floor, and then you could see the muzzle flash and the recoil. You could see him stepping over bodies. Then you could watch more commercials. Murder had been commoditized and repackaged as entertainment that could be digested in five-minute chunks. Dead children sell fast food and probiotic yogurt and web hosting. Dead children move product.

◆ ◆ ◆

Gun sales had risen 300 percent since the shooting. Everyone had guns, even people who didn't have guns.

There were people who said guns were dangerous, that the national obsession with guns is the reason people keep getting killed, that two centuries of gun worship had poisoned our culture, that if we just, once and for all, made a decision to eliminate as many guns as possible then we would all be safer. But guns can't be banned because if guns were banned, then how would we stop people who have guns? If nobody had guns, then how would people use guns? If guns didn't exist, then what would people put in their holsters? If people didn't have guns to put in their holsters, then what would they use to shoot at birds? If people couldn't shoot at birds, not to mention deer and bears and snakes and evil spirits, then wouldn't the world be overrun with birds? With deer and bears and snakes? With evil spirits? If guns were banned, then how would men kill their wives? How would men kill themselves? How would men exact revenge on the world for not giving them everything they'd ever wanted?

I wrote to my congressman with a solution: Instead of manufacturing bulletproof vests and bulletproof glass, because you can't always be in a vest or behind glass, we should begin manufacturing bulletproof children. It will be expensive, but who can put a price on the life of a child? What parent can say, No, I don't want you to be impervious to bullets, I want you to risk your life every day? Instead of banning guns, what they needed to ban was people who get shot. If we stopped having shootable people, then guns wouldn't be such a problem. Guns could be used for their true purpose of killing nonhumans and empty beer cans.

• • •

A month after the shooting, I went back to the gym. I was trying to act normally. Everyone kept saying we needed to get back to normal, to not allow the shooter to change our lives. If we let terror win, then terror wins. This is a country of winners, and one important thing winners don't do is lose. I used to go at least three times a week. Cardio and Pilates and dynamic weightlifting movements. My body was not what I wanted it to be. Every body is a disappointment to its owner, but mine was also a capable and healthy and, viewed in the right light, an attractive body. I looked like a person who could pick things up and move them without help. I looked like a person who could go on a nature hike. But there is no point in having a good body, because bodies are too fragile. No matter what anybody does to ward off death, they will die before they're ready. Thirty minutes of cardio means nothing to the shooter. Bullets can penetrate even the hardest muscles. Working out is a way for us to trick ourselves into thinking we have a chance. I was on the treadmill in the morning and I was running at my normal pace, on an incline, and I was looking away from the TVs where the Republican pundits were blaming the Democrats for the shooting and vice versa and nobody was listening to anybody. I was running and then I heard the door open behind me. Without turning, I saw the shooter pushing through the front door, strapped with bullets and grenades. There were four emergency exits—I had begun taking note of the locations of emergency exits—but they would be wired with explosives, and there was no place I could run. There was no way to be safe and there was no way to be healthy, because health and safety are myths. I had stopped running, and the treadmill belt spit me onto the floor like a tongue rejecting food. Everyone stared at me, and I knew they were thinking: The last thing we need is another crazy person around here.

◆ ◆ ◆

Everywhere in Seldom Falls, people were busy erecting barriers and other safety measures to prevent the occurrence of the thing that had already happened. Even the restaurants were installing metal detectors. Buying a sandwich now meant stripping off your watch and your belt and your jewelry and your shoes and allowing your bag to be X-rayed, and maybe being patted down by a guard before sliding your cash through a slot in bulletproof glass. Everything took so much longer. It was easier just to stay home.

The only places that didn't change were the gun shops.

There, you could still stroll in and plunk down your cash and walk out with a handgun within minutes.

◆ ◆ ◆

One of the problems with living in the friendliest town in America is that people are always being friendly with you. Friendliness is a virtue and friendliness is a weapon. By the time I was in high school, I'd begun to feel stifled by the friendliness. I was fifteen and I went to the pharmacy to drop off a prescription for birth control. The cashier had gone to high school with my father and she called him to ask if he knew what I was up to. He did not know what I was up to, because by this point he'd become detached from himself and would go days without speaking to anyone. He asked my mother and she said she had no idea either, even though it was her suggestion that I acquire birth control pills. My mother was vain and not the sort of person you could rely on. It was very important to her that people perceive her as having what she called a "classy family." The cashier told me to stay there and wait for my father to come pick me up. "You really shouldn't go sneaking around like this," she said. "After everything your father's been through." She reached across the counter for my hand, which I gave her, because I'd been raised to be polite. "I noticed your family hasn't been in church in a while." I barely knew her. The pharmacist looked at my script and shook his head. He had been my softball coach when I was younger. "I can't fill this without one of your parents here," he said, which was not true; I knew that even then. Part of being young is being lied to by adults constantly and being forced to accept it. You can't fight every lie, because then they say you're difficult. And if you're difficult, then they spend all their time trying to fix you. Most of the fixes require more lies. As the pharmacist stared at me and the cashier held my hand, I suddenly felt intense guilt about having a reproductive system. I felt like a deviant for doing what I'd thought was a smart thing.

That night, my mother lectured me about how I'd embarrassed her, and she wouldn't listen when I reminded her that she'd told me to do it. I cried while she yelled at me and I hated that I cried, and that night in my bed I felt the collective eyes of the entire town watching me. I lived in a world with no hiding places. Friendliness engulfed everybody.

◆ ◆ ◆

The sun was still in the bottom of the lake. The township denied this truth, but also encouraged people to bundle up for the foreseeable future. They called it a cold front, but I knew: this is what a limb feels like when it goes necrotic.

Mayor Randy told me to stop calling. He asked me to stop telling people the sun had fallen in the lake. They installed new lights everywhere. Officially, the lights had been installed for safety reasons.

Now everything was too bright. I kept the shades at my house drawn at all times. The endless light drove the owls mad. They dive-bombed cars and attacked civilians and even though the Audubon people were calling it a mystery, it seemed pretty clear: these were bird suicides. The lights were called a temporary measure, but temporary just means not-yet-permanent.

When the Ice Age started, dinosaurs thought it was temporary. Eventually everyone would give up on the sun and accept a life completely dependent on electric light and heaters and synthetic grass and vegetables grown in labs. Because what were we supposed to do, just pick the sun up, strap it into a catapult, and send it back home?

VICTIMS, PART I

SARA R LIVED on my street. I knew her family, but I did not know her well. She was very tall and I sometimes worried that she would get bullied at school, that she would learn to hate herself for her height. By high school, her posture had been ruined because she'd taken to slumping forward to try to fit in. She was in the library during the shooting, and when he burst through the doors, she froze, just feet away from the barrel of his gun.

• • •

Scott L was my neighbor once, back when we were young and lived in the apartments off Main Street, back when everyone in their twenties wanted to live as close as possible to the one so-called vibrant stretch of town. I used to hear him through the walls shouting at sporting events and at video games, but he never shouted at me. He was nice. He was a nice man with a dog and a collection of whimsical ties and a tendency to cover his mouth with his hand when he spoke. People smiled when they saw him. He had been making a soda delivery when the shooting started. He died because he was in the way of a bullet intended for someone else.

· · ·

Colby D lived in the house where I grew up. Two other families had lived there between mine and his, so my presence in the house had long been erased, the drawings on my bedroom ceiling painted over, my buried treasures in the backyard dug up and pawned. I drove past that house often, and I sometimes parked across the street to see what had changed, to try to understand why they replaced the antique wooden front door with an ugly green thing, why they'd removed my father's stained-glass window from the parlor, why they had ripped out the tree I'd twice tried to climb and from which I'd twice fallen, twice breaking my left wrist. This was an unhappy place and still I loved it and felt protective of it. I wanted it to be exactly what I'd remembered, because I wanted to feel justified in my adolescent anger and loneliness, but the house gradually became a stranger. Time doesn't just change the way we look or the way we feel, it changes our insides and turns us into entirely new people. The past can be vicious, but at least it's a terror you already know.

When they showed Colby's face on the news, I felt like a stepbrother had died. My own brother had nearly died many times, and each time I felt like God himself had reached down my throat and started squeezing my lungs. In his picture, Colby looked cocky and self-assured and frustratingly handsome. He looked like a boy whom the other boys would listen to. His mother had abandoned him when he was young, but his father was a kind man and generous and he loved his children. When I watched them working together in their backyard, I saw every one of his motions was filled with the kind of love I didn't really believe existed until I saw it in person. I drove away before they could see me, but then I spent the rest of the day thinking: There are kind men in the world and they are good and his son will be kind also. You form bonds with people for all kinds of reasons and sometimes the reason is that that person lives in a place where you used to live, and sometimes you can lie in bed and transport yourself back to that place and try to get inside his head and feel in some way connected.

◆ ◆ ◆

Katie O worked in the science department. She claimed to have a disease that made her bones weaker than other people's bones, but she provided no documentation. She said the monthly treat of pizza in the teachers' lounge was discriminatory because she was allergic to garlic. The students loved her because she often napped through class, asking them to quietly read their books. She was unpleasant and unreliable, and at parent-teacher conferences she talked mostly about her weak bones. More than a few of us thought she was hiding an addiction to something. Did this mean she deserved to be shot? It did not mean she deserved to be shot. When I was seven, I read a book about a boy named Even Steven, and I became obsessed with the idea of fairness. I shouted at my parents and my friends and my teachers that things were not fair: bedtimes, being forced to eat peas, not being allowed to have a salamander as a pet, having to help my father do yard work. One day, while I was wailing about some injustice, my father grabbed me by the arm and said, "Nothing's fair. Nothing has ever been fair. You don't hear me whining about it all the time." Sometimes people get shot, and most of them don't deserve it, not in the cosmic-justice sense. But the idea of cosmic justice itself is misguided.

◆ ◆ ◆

Cameron T was unattractive like his uncle Patrick, who had briefly been the most popular kid in my high school class. You're not supposed to say it when the kids are ugly, but some of them are. At sixteen, Cameron's uncle Patrick was able to grow a beard to hide his angular, asymmetrical face. By senior year, he had a full lumberjack's beard, and his hair was long enough to hang over his eyes. He played guitar and was the lead singer in two different bands that played gigs at out-of-town bars and hung out all night using fake IDs. He bought the beer for every party I ever went to. He was unpredictable and hard to trust; one day he would love you and say you were his only real friend and the next he would be onstage singing a song about how he wished you were dead. Later he was diagnosed as bipolar, but at the time, we just thought he was cruel. After a year of college, he joined the army and we all assumed he'd come back straightened out and in the best shape of his life, but he went AWOL after three months. The next time I heard about him, he was living in a trailer in the desert in Arizona with three other people and two dogs. They were distributing canned goods to illegal immigrants. I saw him only a year or two ago, and he looked washed out, wispy, ground down. He told me he'd moved back to town near his family and was living on disability, spending most of his days posting videos of himself playing guitar online. Most recently, he posted two videos—one was an elegy for Cameron that is frankly not very good, and the other was a folk song about how we need to kill all the killers before the killers kill us first.

• • •

Kirk B got a seventeen-line obituary in the local paper. It focused on his public service, first as an air force pilot, and later as a volunteer firefighter. None of the lines mentioned the strange pleasure he took in shooting squirrels with a BB gun, or the brief period when we all suspected he was living in his car in the parking lot and shaving over the sink in the teachers' lounge. Probably it's not relevant to an obituary to mention those things. I'm not sure what obituaries are for. You can tell people's stories, but nothing you do is complete or accurate. It's just a list of people they used to know and jobs they used to do. We spend so much time trying to be effective mourners, but we have no idea how to do it. Even elephants are better at mourning.

JUNE

EIGHT WEEKS AFTER the shooting, I got an email from a man who called himself Patriot Paul and who said, "I'm going to show up at your house one night when you're not expecting it and I'm going to cut your whore mouth open with my bowie knife and fill it up with dicks. I'm going to cover you in dicks and smother you with them and when you're dead I'll hang you over my mantel like a trophy."

I wrote back and asked him where he gets all those extra dicks, and is there a wholesaler nearby because I could use a few spares.

I got emails like this frequently. Middle-aged men saw news of the shooting and thought: The world needs me now. They put on their capes and swooped in to the rescue, but when they got there, they found out they had no superpowers. They were just sad men in capes. So they got angry and looked for a woman to blame. They were terrified and they wanted to dress it up as courage, and they spewed hate into the world in hopes of drown-

43

ing out the threats. They demanded explanations and then before anyone had a chance to explain, offered their own theories.

The shooter's mother had to explain herself to a dozen different news anchors, who all asked her questions like, *Where do you think you went wrong?* and *What advice do you have for mothers out there who don't want their sons to turn out like yours* and *Do you have a message for the grieving families?* She had to beg forgiveness for having birthed a boy she didn't understand. The pundits said she had feminized the boy, that she had made him wear dresses when he was younger (they were Halloween costumes, she said, and it was only twice), that she had allowed him to go vegetarian and to quit the football team when he was ten. Could the boy have been saved by joining a couple sports clubs? Would he have been better off if he'd been adopted? Are some children just born evil?

The shooter's mother had a name, though the media rarely used it. She became simply The Mother Of. He had robbed her of her right to define herself. Her name was Sylvia. An elegant name, the name of a VP of marketing or a conceptual artist with a small but enthusiastic following. She was tall and papery and rustled in the wind. She looked like an old rocker past her prime. She had excellent posture.

She was two years younger than me. We'd grown up in the part of town everyone called the Mud Flats. People thought we were poor, because we were, but not as poor as they said. I rarely spoke to her because she was younger than me and people said she was weird. She missed school frequently and always seemed to be sick. When I was in eighth grade and she was in sixth, a couple of boys in my class got in the habit of tormenting her by pulling her hair, throwing candy down her shirt, tossing her books out the bus window. Before the end of that school year, she was gone, and I later learned she had moved away to live with her grandparents while her parents got themselves sorted out. When she came back her father was gone. In high school she had a reputation for acting crazy, for taking dares from anyone, and sometimes turning up in random beds on Saturday mornings. She liked to party, but why should I have cared? Everybody liked to party. What else was there to do?

• • •

About a year before the shooting, I saw Sylvia in the movie theater. She was there by herself and I was there by myself, and I sat next to her because I wasn't comfortable being alone. We were seeing a big new action film about a young cop single-handedly stopping a drug cartel. We saw more than three hundred people killed on the screen. She reached over and held my hand. Her hand was cold and flaky and I felt like if I pulled hard enough I could tear it off her arm. When the movie ended, she applauded, and afterward she kept telling me how great it was. She invited me out for coffee or wine. I wasn't sure I wanted to talk to her much more. Her eyes never stopped moving and she chewed on her bottom lip. She didn't want to go to her own home. Before I left, she said, "Do you ever have kids at the school who say they hate their parents?" I told her that's the only thing some of them are capable of saying. When I was their age, I worked at hating my parents harder than I did on any other task. Teenagers would eat hate if they could.

"But do you think they get better?" she said.

"I don't understand the first thing about kids," I said. It wasn't until much later that I remembered that night, and thought about how I could have been inside the house, just down the hall from the boy as he was already plotting his murders. How I could have sat there with his mother and maybe she would even have told me something about how terrifying her son was. How she had nowhere to hide from him.

♦ ♦ ♦

Everywhere around town, people were remembering their own brushes with the greatest villain we'd ever seen. I remembered the time I saw him at work with his mother at the dry cleaner. Some days he sat behind the counter doing homework. There was no one else at home to take care of him so he had to stay with Sylvia while she worked. He was twelve then, the age when the police say he was already writing vile things on the Internet. He handed me my blouses. He smiled at me and he shook my hand.

Once he'd murdered people, we were forced to account for him, to carve out a space in our brains where he would always live. I could see how this would appeal to him.

♦ ♦ ♦

I saw Sylvia only one time after the shooting, at a gas station, where we'd both gone overnight to buy milk. Infamy makes grocery stores difficult, but gas station attendants don't ask questions at two a.m.; they stand quietly and hope not to get robbed. Sylvia paid for my milk and apologized for what her son had done. I could see even then she was dying. She followed me to my car apologizing again and again, and then she collapsed into my chest. I held on to her and kept her on her feet. The last time I'd had an experience like this in a parking lot was with a girl out celebrating her twenty-first birthday. She'd broken the heel on her shoe and had fallen to her knees in tears between two parked cars because she was too drunk to handle the stress of aging. I gave that girl my shoes, and she hurled herself at me the same way Sylvia had. She held on to me and I held on to her and she cried. It's the moral thing to keep holding on as long as the other person needs it. It's a way of affirming that we're human. You can try to hug a cat but eventually you'll feel its claws.

◆ ◆ ◆

I got an email from an ex. "I don't blame you for what happened," he said. My life was now about seeking forgiveness for things I hadn't done. Maybe that's how it always had been; apologizing just in case I'd done something wrong, assuming I'd done a bad thing even if nobody knew what it was. He also wanted me to know I looked great in the pictures they'd been showing on the news, and maybe would I want to catch up sometime? "I'm sure you could use a friend," he said.

The ex was named was Robert but he liked to be called Robbie. Robbie is the name of a boy, a kid who wears his ball cap backward and sits in the bleachers at baseball games sneaking cigarettes and spilling beer on bystanders as he jostles for foul balls. Robbie is not the name of an adult man who is ready to live with an adult woman. But he was very pretty. He was ten years younger than me, and he had hair the color of Nilla Wafers and skin like fondant and I had dreams about eating him. I didn't think I would ever get to date a boy his age again.

We'd first met at a coffee shop. Robbie was standing in line behind me. The barista was young and overwhelmed. She was panicking, so I offered to help her. I was more helpful in those days. I told her she needed to do something dramatic to make a statement. She then tried to push the espresso machine off the counter and it barely budged. I leaned over and helped her, and together we knocked it to the floor. The sound was exactly like that of an espresso machine crashing onto the floor. The girl started crying. She sank to the floor and tried to hide beneath the counter. Robbie tapped me on the shoulder and said, "You should probably get out of here." I followed him to his car and then we went to a different coffee shop and somewhere in there I kissed him.

When we were dating, Robbie was incapable of having an honest conversation with me until he was drunk. When he wanted to get serious, he would always have three or four more drinks than I did. I drank less then than I do now. At that time, I didn't really appreciate the benefits of intoxication. I was still under the impression that drinking had to be conducted socially. Most of our dates started awkwardly and tentatively, then turned nice for two hours before he switched to gin and tonic, and then he got sloppy and started talking too much. If I suggested he drink some water, he'd get suddenly defensive. Then in the morning he would wake up and say, "That last drink really hit me hard," which was his way of apologizing.

He owned a collection of interesting pint glasses with boring origin stories. He chewed sunflower seeds compulsively because his doctor told him he needed more salt in his diet, and he spit the shells into an oversized plastic cup that stood on his table for weeks before he emptied it. I did laundry for him on weekends.

I sat across from Robbie in a diner booth, knowing everyone in the room was looking at me. He removed his hat, which I took to mean he was about to do something sincere. He reached across the table and held my hand. I was afraid he was going to propose to me. "This whole thing has been really bringing me down," he said. He squeezed my hand and pulled it closer. "It's just like . . . It makes you think."

"What does?" I said. I knew what he meant, but I was tired of him not just saying what he meant. I was annoyed by the thudding dullness of the way people had talked about the killings, the practiced frowns and the miserable acceptance. There had to be a better way.

"You know. The whole big thing."

"The shooting?" I said. "At the school? The school shooting?"

He let go of my hand. "Come on," he said. "You know what I mean."

He pulled his phone out of his pocket and tapped out a message to someone. He looked down at it for another minute. I felt the weight of my own phone in my pocket, demanding

I check it. Each time my phone buzzed, I thought it could be Calvin. Before the shooting, Calvin and I were on a schedule of three or four phone calls a year, and now he wanted to talk every week. He kept sending me messages saying he was worried about me. He didn't understand that his worry only made me feel worse, because I knew I was inflicting my unhappiness on him. Robbie reached across the table again. "Look. Listen. I'm trying here, okay?"

Robbie wanted me to congratulate him for being sad about a mass murder. Men want to be rewarded for having emotions. They think it's an accomplishment to have sincere thoughts and feel sad about things.

When we left the coffee shop, we picked up a bottle of vodka and returned to his apartment. We drank for a long time and at some point we were both crying and then I was demanding that he fuck me and then he was inside me, and then he wasn't, and then I felt sick from the alcohol.

In the morning, he tapped me on the shoulder and said, "I have a surprise for you." I was not looking for any more surprises in my life. He presented me with a platter of bacon, toast, eggs. He didn't stand there waiting for me to thank him the way he might have back when we lived together; he just performed the nice gesture and then allowed it to exist.

Eggs are chickens that haven't been born yet. You eat them and then inside you they are born and your body is filled with birds. If you eat too many, your stomach bursts open and the birds escape and fill the sky above your body.

I picked at the eggs and said thank you.

◆ ◆ ◆

I remembered while I was lying in Robbie's bed that it was Calvin's son's birthday. Calvin had two children—a four-year-old boy named Harlan and a two-year-old girl named Colleen. I had only met Harlan once, at his christening. I was his godmother, for reasons I never understood. I remember standing in the church next to the baptismal font and fearing the whole time the priest would ask me to explain myself. The sacraments are supposed to fill you with grace, to make you feel God's love. I felt exposed in the priest's presence, judged by the hovering Christ in the stained-glass window behind the altar. They say Jesus ascended to heaven, but nobody ever saw where he went. You're supposed to have faith, but nothing is more dangerous than faith. That day was the only time I had ever seen Calvin's new home in his new city. I had never met his daughter, though I'd seen the pictures. I had met his wife a few times before that. He'd been introduced to Nina by a friend after one of his meetings. She was a social worker with a degree in library science, a sleeve of tattoos, and a tiny stud in her nose, and in the most recent pictures I'd seen, she had green hair. She looked very cool. She looked like someone who knew about interesting movie festivals and who could get backstage at concerts. I was certain she didn't like me.

On Harlan's birthday, it was my job to send a card with a $50 check. It was my job to call Calvin and ask him to put Harlan on the phone so I could wish him happy birthday while he stood in silence, confused like most children by what he was supposed to say to someone on the phone. According to the priest, I was also supposed to provide spiritual guidance to him. I texted Calvin to say I was a little hung up but I would call later, and he responded right away. "We don't ask for much," he wrote.

• • •

Robbie kissed me on the top of my head and said, "Babe, stop crying." Was I crying? "I'll take care of you." His apartment still looked like a college dorm room. The backward hat and gym shorts, which looked fine on him in his mid-twenties, now seemed like a sad affectation of youth. I don't think he wanted to take care of me so much as he wanted me to tell him how safe he made me feel. He rarely wore shirts indoors, and though his body was not as beautiful as it had once been, I still wanted nothing more than to feel it on top of me, to be pressed so close to me that our skins melted together.

"I have to go," I said.

"Right now?"

I took his spare key and said, "I'll bring this back."

• • •

TIME TO HEAL, the newspaper headline said. It read like an order. The community was tired of sympathizing. The bodies had been buried. The prayer services and vigils had been conducted. The speeches from politicians. The threats of copycat attacks. The benefit concert. It had been two months. Everyone wanted to move on. There were other things to worry about.

We all had lives with real issues and problems before the

shooting. And those things were still there, unchanged, except for this one big thing we were supposed to be getting over and we couldn't. It occluded everything like a cataract.

"Do you remember when everything used to be simple?" a woman at the bus stop asked me.

JULY

'D BECOME SUSPICIOUS of knocks on my door, so when I heard a knock my first instinct was to dive behind my couch.

The knocking persisted. I crawled toward the door then stood to look through the peephole. On the other side of the door, I saw Angie Sparks.

Angie used to work as a clerk at the high school. Five years ago, she'd gone back to school to get a business degree and opened a small clothing boutique downtown. I hadn't thought about her since the grand opening of her shop. Back then, she was really into Buddhism. Her shop was full of items that could be vaguely described as spiritual. Now she was something else.

"Anna," she said when I opened the door. "Have you found Jesus yet?"

"I've been looking all over for him, but can't turn him up."

"You're letting your cynicism blind you."

I was hoping my cynicism would be the thing that kept me alive.

"May I have permission to enter your home?" Angie said.

"You're not a vampire are you? Because you have to tell me. Otherwise it's entrapment." Not even a smirk.

Angie reached into the breast pocket of her jacket—everyone was wearing jackets now, with the sun gone—and I was sure she was reaching for a gun. Every day, I saw people making sudden moves and then the shooting flashed by in tiny explosions in my brain. I saw the shooter with the gun stalking the halls, and I heard the children screaming for help and I tasted the blood on my tongue. I sometimes saw myself with the gun, jolting backward when I pulled the trigger. I traced his steps through the school, banging on lockers and laughing and firing wildly in the air like a western bandit. The shooter tore through the gauzy curtain of security that made me think I was in a safe place, that made me think there was some way I could live without fear. I saw John K seeing the gun and running toward it, putting himself between the bullets and the students. He was a hero, and being a hero didn't make him any less dead.

"I'd like you to read this," Angie said. "And I'd like to talk to you about it." It was a pamphlet about the apocalypse titled *Signs Preceding the End of the World*.

I told her if we were going to do this, I would need a drink.

• • •

Was it brunch time? Was it Sunday? I had a mimosa and I had some kind of egg dish sitting in front of me. When the waiter asked me how I was doing today, I said I was fine. He said he was also fine. Angie was fine too. Everybody was fine.

"Time is running short," Angie said. "You need to repent and accept Christ into your life." She'd said this several times already. She was very big on repenting.

"Does the Repent Now thing ever actually work for recruiting?" I said.

"I mean. No. Not really. But it should."

I sliced my eggs open and watched the yolk run like blood over the hash browns. "Do you think Jesus has a gun?"

"I don't see why he wouldn't." Angie sipped her mimosa. I'd thought evangelicals didn't drink alcohol, but maybe Angie hadn't committed fully yet. Or maybe there were exceptions for recruiting trips. "He probably has a whole mess of guns, because how else would he fight off Satan?"

"Satan has guns too?"

"And tanks, probably."

Angie told me I was in limbo. She said once I accepted that Jesus would save me from myself, I would feel decades of unhappiness lifted from me. I would be weightless and ascend to a higher plane. She told me a parable about a mole and a duck. But I wasn't interested in parables. I was not a mole or a duck. I was a person with a real problem. Parables are for children.

◆ ◆ ◆

I'd seen people panic about the end times before. For six months leading up to Y2K, my father had mailed me newspaper clippings about our impending doom. He never included a note, though sometimes he drew smiley faces next to the headlines. Calvin sometimes spent the night at my apartment to get away from them, and he said the house was filling up with canned goods. My father wanted to be ready. My mother didn't care enough to stop him. After it happened—after nothing happened—my father's notes stopped. My mother, I was told, opened the cans one by one and poured them into the sink, the garbage disposal running nonstop through the night.

Part of me wanted to laugh at Angie. Part of me knew the moment you start screaming that the end is near, your life becomes entirely about death. But this time felt different. I read the pamphlet and I thought: Why not? Why wouldn't the world end now? It has to end eventually. Why shouldn't we be the ones to see it?

The pamphlet named all the usual signs of apocalypse— flooding, wildlife rebellion, fires, rampant shootings, amorality— and included lots of frightening line graphs. There was also the sun to think about. That seemed like a very scientific reason to give up on the future. In other cities, the sun was still there. It didn't make sense, but there's no reason anything ever has to make sense. We're the ones who try to force sense onto the world.

According to the literature, the end would look like a movie— a sudden darkness, a portal from hell, demons pouring out, a bloody battle between the forces of good and evil. "You might want to make this sound less exciting," I said. "I kind of want to not repent just so I can see the whole scene."

"I think you're missing the point."

"Make it sound boring. People don't want to be bored."

Angie snatched the pamphlet away. "I don't deserve to be

mocked for my beliefs," she said. "I am a person. I vote. I speak to Jesus every night." She emptied her glass. "What do *you* do?"

• • •

My house was still in disarray. I'd never considered myself an orderly person, but I had never lived in such a mess before. I knew my house needed to be cleaned, but the thought of starting the job overwhelmed me. My mother believed a clean house was a sign of a clean soul. She cleaned my room while I was out and I dirtied it to spite her, and by the time I was eighteen she'd given up on both me and my soul.

• • •

My family used to go to church every week. My mother made us dress up, even though Catholics didn't care how you dressed. Showing up to church in Seldom Falls is a good way to advertise yourself to the community as happy and well adjusted. I never knew if anybody believed in what we were doing on Sundays. My father sang the hymns out of tune, and he kept his eyes closed the whole time he sang. Calvin sat next to me and my mother sat next to Calvin, and when Father Graham told us to sit, we sat. When he told us to kneel, we knelt. I read the hymnals and memorized the songs. My mother never took communion. Calvin never prayed. Every Christmas, we went to the midnight mass, and it would get so crowded with half-drunk, lonely people that the air in the room became oppressive. Most years, I passed out from the heat. My mother thought this was a sign of my religious fervor. When I woke up, she would be smiling at me, saying, "I always knew you had a saint inside you." One time when I passed out, my head hit the pew in front of me. That's why I have a scar above my eye. A man told me once he thought it was sexy and mysterious. He traced it with his finger. He said, "I love a woman with scars."

· · ·

After eleven weeks, the investigation of the shooter was officially closed. The manifesto he'd written had told them everything, particularly who he hated and why. It was a list depressing in its banality, in its adolescent conviction that he'd discovered some grand truth about how people are phonies, how organized religion corrupts, how the world is mostly about pain. As if we didn't all know this, as if we also weren't trying to find ways to deal with it that didn't involve murder. In his manifesto, he talked about loneliness as if that problem had been invented to torment him alone. He talked about being smarter than everyone else. He talked about wanting to open people's eyes to all the terrible things he'd learned online. If you spend too much time online without stepping away, it's like stepping into the midday sun with dilated pupils. There is too much to take in and no way to process everything, and all you know is that it hurts and you need to get away. We're supposed to be gradually exposed to the world's horrors so that over time we can develop an immunity. We learn about failure and loss and cruelty and rejection and inferiority in a sequence; if you hit a kid with all of that at once, how is he going to survive? He'd left everything piled on a dresser in his bedroom, along with a picture he'd asked them to use on the news, in which he'd posed with his arms crossed over his chest, pistols in each hand, like he was on the poster for a war movie.

The shooter had a name and a face and a past. Everyone knows his name and face and select parts of his past, but what they didn't talk about was that the shooter was a boy. He was a boy in a world in which boys play by pretending to kill other boys, he was a boy with access to military-grade firepower but not to an adult support system or psychiatric services. Boys kill and they kill and they kill and then they kill again. Boys are made of snails and puppy-dog tails and pipe bombs and semiautomatic rifles. Girls are made of sugar and spice and who knows what else. Their anatomy is a mystery.

◆ ◆ ◆

What did I want to be when I was young? I wanted to be a very tall person. I wanted to be a robot with the power to self-destruct. I wanted to be a lizard lying on a rock and sticking its tongue out lazily while other animals steered clear of me. I wanted to be the moon and only show parts of myself and go into hiding periodically and control the tides. I wanted to flood cities and reflect the sun back onto everyone. I wanted to be something people aspired to.

◆ ◆ ◆

Before I went back to college, Calvin's addiction had already taken over his life, and ours. Even though I was an hour away at school, his problems bled into my world. My mother called to complain about him every day, and every time she kicked him out of the house, he stayed in my dorm. My roommate hated the idea of having a strange man sleeping on the floor of her room, and she knew just from looking at him that he was an addict. Everyone has terrible compulsions, but most people can hide them, quarantine them to specific, safe areas of their life. The third time he slept there, he stole jewelry from my roommate, and I was kicked out of campus housing. I've never been able to say no to him. When he was eleven, I would buy beer for him and his friends on weekends, and I was the first one to give him pot. Back then, it was very important to me that he see me as a cool older sister. I felt I owed him, because his life had been too hard already, and too much of it was my fault. Even if I had known it would escalate the way it did, I might still have done everything the same way. It's a mistake to look at your past and imagine alternate outcomes, because time machines don't exist, and even if they did, only the rich could afford them. I decided to be a teacher because of Calvin, because I was still idealistic then, and thought I could make amends for him by saving other children. In my life, I have never been more committed to anything than I was to teaching at age twenty-three. For a few years, I even did it very well.

• • •

Robbie asked me to take a bike ride with him. He said we both needed more fresh air. "You look like you haven't been outside in a year," he said. Outside, I reminded him, is where you go to get killed. "God," he said. "You're always so, what's the word?" I did not know the word. "Starts with an *m*. You know what I mean."

I wore a helmet and he didn't. I figured I should control the variables I could control. You can't stop a shooter from rampaging. But you can wear a helmet in case you fall off a bike and hit your head on a rock.

Robbie was a natural athlete. He'd played two sports in college and bounced when he walked. He never looked more comfortable in the world than he did when he was running or biking or swimming or dribbling a ball. He had to keep slowing down to let me catch up, but I preferred the view from last place, enjoyed seeing him so competent and capable and physically impressive. The muscular bulge of his calves, the tension in his hamstrings and the sculpted lines of his arms braced on the handlebars. Since I was a child, I've admired men who are supremely competent at minor tasks: my father sawing wood precisely, my brother dicing an onion in seconds, my first boyfriend flying a model airplane through an obstacle course. My mind emptied. I pedaled with the thoughtless momentum of a machine. My legs are machines and they pump up and down and they carry me where I tell them to. My arms are bone and flesh and blood and ligaments and they are tools I use to pick things up, to balance myself, to push things away. My heart is an engine that ignites and propels me forward even when I don't want to be propelled.

We'd been riding for about an hour and I needed a break. We were a few miles out of town on a nature trail that connected a Civil War battlefield to a memorial from a different war. We propped our bikes against a tree. "I should have brought a picnic or something," he said. "My bad."

I had told him many times that I don't need romance and

I'm not interested in being courted. But a picnic sounded nice. The thought of him thinking of it, even belatedly, was nice. My shirt clung sweaty to my breasts and I shivered in the breeze. The grass rustled near us and I was sure, for a moment, that it was a snake, that I was about to feel its fangs in my calf and that would be that. It felt like decades ago since I'd last been able to enjoy something.

It was not a snake, it was a bunny, hopping away wide-eyed. A hawk circled overhead and contemplated swooping down on the moving target. Somewhere not far, there was a fox hiding and waiting for a scared rabbit to come scampering into its jaws.

"Your nose is bleeding again," Robbie said.

◆ ◆ ◆

A week before the bike ride, I'd woken up with blood smeared across my pillow and on my face, and I was sure I'd been murdered overnight. When Robbie saw the blood-encrusted pillowcase, he nearly vomited, and then he told me I needed to see a doctor. The body needs to process the trauma too. I stopped wearing white shirts, and started carrying a handkerchief in my back pocket. I dripped trails of blood all over Robbie's apartment.

◆ ◆ ◆

In the grocery store, I was hustling to fill my cart with canned goods—I thought this would be step one to building a bomb shelter—and a young woman grabbed my arm. She leaned in close and whispered, "Is he here?"

I thought she was another evangelical. I thought she was

talking about Jesus. "I'm not really sure. Isn't he supposed to be everywhere?" I said.

"You can get help," she said.

"I've read the pamphlets, sure."

She squeezed my arm. "I'm serious. Take this," she said, stuffing a business card in my hip pocket. "I've been there." She wouldn't let go until I made eye contact with her and promised to call the number on the card. As she walked away, I tasted a drop of blood in the corner of my mouth and then I understood how I looked. There are days when you feel like the whole world is staring at you but they're not, and then there are the other days. The card she'd given me was for a shelter for battered women.

Later, I told Robbie about the misunderstanding. "Why are you laughing at that?" he said. "How could it possibly be funny that people think I'm beating you?" He never really appreciated my jokes.

◆ ◆ ◆

Through the first few months, I tried to have my breakdowns in private. Did I even have a right to mourn a mass killing that didn't kill anyone I loved? I wasn't there to witness it, but I still wake up and feel it, convinced it's the only thing I've ever seen. I will have a drink in the afternoon and then I will think about how I could have been there, and maybe I should have been there. I never had any desire to be a hero, or a martyr, but wouldn't everyone have been better off if I'd been killed instead? It was the only thing I thought about. My ears only heard gunshots. My lungs were full of bullets. One is meant to be stoic after a tragic event—if tragic is even the right word. One should keep calm, et cetera.

While waiting for a latte, I heard the barista call my name and I waited so he could call again because I wanted to hear my name expressed publicly and loudly and without judgment. I wanted to hear my name and affirm that I existed. And then before I could take the latte, I felt a wave of gratitude so powerful it broke me in half, and then I felt guilt for feeling good in the wake of a tragedy, if tragedy is even the right word. But to have a stranger talk to me like a normal person and to be polite and even smile at me was such a relief.

HOW TO BE SAFE, PART I

EVERY NIGHT BEFORE bed, make sure all your windows and doors are locked. Blow out every candle. Turn off your stove and your oven. Check outlets and light switches for loose connections. Cut strategic holes in the drywall to inspect for black mold. Search your toilet for stowaway snakes. Check your windows again. Set up a series of booby traps between your bed and the front door. Pray to whichever god is most likely to protect you from harm. Make peace with the ghosts in your home. Remove all suffocation hazards from the vicinity of your bed. There should be no plastic bags near your bed. Keep a phone on your bedside table pre-dialed to 911. Take a sleeping pill so you can get through the night, but don't take too many. In the morning, check your windows again.

NEVER GO ONLINE. Online there are hordes of bored teenagers who want to terrorize you for laughs. There are angry young men who fantasize about flaying you and inserting themselves into you and desecrating you (the joke is on them: the body is not sacred; it can't be desecrated). There are lonely adults who sit like snipers waiting for the perfect moment to destroy you. There are identity thieves, who will wear you like a mask and then discard you so someone else can find you at the bottom of a trash can. Never go online, because if you go online, you'll never be able to hide again. But also never go outside. Try to find a way to live on a plane of existence inaccessible to the rest of the world.

GET YOURSELF SOME MONEY. As much as you can. Money is insulation. Money allows you to go to a doctor regularly and eat food that is made out of food. Money helps you live in places far away from danger. Money buys security systems and guard dogs and walls and moats. Money buys the legal right to shoot people who look scary. There are walls within walls that you can only see if you have enough money. Money buys an elaborate funeral. When you're dead, you get to keep your three most valuable items from life, so that when you're in heaven you can be sure everyone knows still that you were rich on Earth, that even here you're not somebody to mess with.

TRY TO GROW WINGS. Spend your days thinking birdlike thoughts. Watch videos of birds in flight. Communicate exclusively via chirps and squawks. Eventually, if you're lucky, you will feel the nubs of the wings sprouting like crocus buds peeking above the springtime soil. When you can fly, you can avoid the terrors of land-based travel and shelter yourself in the tallest trees. As long as you're bigger than an eagle, you will have no natural predators in the sky. But no matter how high you fly, how much you conceal your nest, there will always be men on the ground with guns and bullets and the desire to destroy your muscle and tendons and ligaments with those bullets. They will camouflage themselves and hide for days in trees just for the chance to kill you and stuff you with polyurethane foam and then mount you on their walls. You are a trophy. You are a story a man can tell while he smokes a cigar with his buddies.

AUGUST

BOMB THREATS CLOSED down most of Seldom Falls one afternoon. A suspicious package was found at the corner of Main
and Buttonwood. A suspicious car was parked at the end of the
200 block of Cherry Avenue. A dark-skinned individual was seen
acting suspiciously in front of Holmes' Pharmacy. Most of the
calls about suspicious activity in town were about dark-skinned
men, even though the shooter himself had been a pale white boy.
The most dangerous thing someone could do was walk through
Seldom Falls with a different skin color. The dark-skinned man
at the pharmacy was surrounded by SWAT teams. The police
rolled down Main Street in a military ATV. There were bomb-
detecting robots. There was a controlled explosion. The man was
detained and questioned on suspicion of terroristic activity. Later,
when they released him, he had to move to a new town because
the people here still believed he was guilty. I watched it all from
behind the police barrier. I saw the snipers on the roof. I prepared to feel the shrapnel under my skin, to take on the suffering

of others. Not to be a hero but to fit in. At that time, I still had delusions of importance. I thought being bombed would inspire something in somebody. Around the perimeter, men cocked their guns, waiting for the opportunity to kill an authentic bad guy.

Seldom Falls had increased the size of the police force by 50 percent since the shooting. They put recruits in an accelerated training program, and they waived the background check for anyone who could pass the written test on the first try. Officers with little training were armed and ready to protect. To serve.

Arrests skyrocketed. This was cited as evidence of improvement. Trials were expedited so people could go to jail faster. Periodically, Mayor Randy announced that they had reason to believe there was a credible threat to Seldom Falls, though he could not tell us what kind of threat or how he knew. He told us to act normally. Acting strangely would allow the terrorists to win. Everyone had become obsessed with this game we were playing with terrorists; we'd started counting our wins and losses like sports fans, though nobody could agree what counted as a win or a loss. He told us to also be wary of strangers and to immediately report any suspicious behavior. Later, they would announce someone had been detained and we had been saved from another attack.

Nobody knew why, but after decades of relative safety, our township was under siege.

· · ·

I was sixteen the last time Seldom Falls had endured a major crisis, when the lake overflowed and flooded half the town. It was the end of winter; the snow mounds on the side of the road were tall enough that I couldn't see over most of them. It rained for ten straight days, melting the snow and saturating everything within a mile radius of the lake. Our house was just outside the areas that got the worst damage, but our basement flooded; and Calvin and I were hauling buckets full of water outside, pointlessly, all day. For every bucket we dumped outside, the same amount of water was pouring in through our foundation. Calvin was too young to be helpful for long. He got tired and his hands callused, and my mother screamed at him to hustle before we lost everything. "Why don't you make yourself useful?" she yelled. He dropped his full bucket on the living-room floor and went outside to cry in the yard. My father was not home, but when Calvin cried he hid in the yard so he wouldn't be yelled at for being too sensitive. We didn't know where my father was during the flood. My mother ran to her bedroom and changed into a swimsuit, then dove into the murky water, searching for something. She emerged like some kind of monster, hugging a ruined cardboard box against her body. I went outside to find Calvin and rub his back until he calmed down and caught his breath, until he felt comfortable enough to go back inside. Later, I sneaked into my mother's bedroom to see what was in the box: there was a Bible and a rosary blessed by the archbishop. There were two photos of her and my father when they were young and optimistic and had perfect skin. Everyone has to hold on to at least one picture like that so they can prove they existed. So they can say, "I wasn't always like this."

The flood destroyed about a hundred homes and seriously

damaged a lot more. Eight people died, and the hospitals over-flowed with injured and sick people. It was the kind of disaster people would talk about for the rest of their lives. Classes at the high school were canceled for three weeks so students and faculty could help clear rubble. It was the hardest I had ever worked in my life. We spent days picking through the remains of our neighbors' homes looking for anything salvageable. Later they asked us to give blood, and I did, despite my reservations. In a room full of my classmates, I lay on the tiny bed while the phlebotomist rubbed iodine on my arm and reassured me that it wouldn't be so bad, just a little pinch and a burning sensation. And at first it wasn't bad, it was just a little pinch and a burning sensation, but then I looked at my arm and I saw the blood flow-ing out of me and all I wanted was to push it all back into my veins. I tried to panic quietly, but now I felt trapped and terrified, and I thought they would let my blood keep draining until I was completely empty. The phlebotomist stopped by and looked at my bag, and said, "Wow, you're a slow bleeder." I rocked in the bed and I tried to keep repeating to myself the details of cellu-lar reproduction, which we'd been learning before the flood. I quizzed myself on the differences between eukaryotes and pro-karyotes, and I tried to remember how viruses fit into the picture. I tried not to turn into a virus while I waited. At some point the phlebotomist freed me, and I vowed never to donate again. But six years later, Calvin was in the hospital after taking a terrible beating from someone, and I was lying down again, the blood again swirling out of my arm and into the bags and soon into my brother's body. Your blood is one of the only things you truly own, and yet they can take it out of you. They can put it in other people. They can combine people in any way they want. Traces of my blood are still inside Calvin today.

• • •

In another safe town across the country, another boy with a gun and a grudge shot a classroom full of children. He didn't even know them. He'd been dumped by a girl at his high school and he wanted to prove to her that he was important. He left a note blaming her. He was hoping to set the record for kills, but he'd never fired a gun before and his aim was poor. Five people died. Four were wounded. The safe town is dark now. It is cold and will never feel safe again.

In America we send children to school to get shot and to learn algebra and physics and history and biology and literature. Less civilized nations don't have such an organized system for murdering their children. Mass murders in undeveloped countries occur because they are savages. Mass murders occur in our country because we are self-actualized and recognize the importance of occasional virgin sacrifices. Those other countries have to stage civil wars and conscript the children into the army and keep them high on meth and give them AK-47s, and this system is all around less predictable and not nearly as safe for the adults. They need famine and poverty to slowly choke children to death, rather than humanely shooting them at their desks. They need predator drones dispatched by a nation significantly more advanced in child-killing.

American children know someday they may grow up to be

good guys and once that occurs, they will want to live in a world in which good guys are still capable of stopping bad guys. The children learn how to hide beneath their desks. They spend every morning learning what to do in the case of an active shooter. The students are like bulletproof vests for the rest of society. We only feel unsafe because we're actually safer than anyone else on the planet.

◆ ◆ ◆

Most days, there were rallies downtown. Anti-gun rallies and pro-gun rallies. Rallies to increase awareness and treatment of mental illness. Anti-immigration rallies. Anti-Muslim rallies. There were always crowds shuffling around in the heart of Seldom Falls, a mass of people angry about something and holding signs in the air. Police helicopters hovered overhead. They weren't in a position to do anything. If I'd been mugged, a helicopter would have been useless. On the ground, the police wore riot gear and carried military-grade weaponry that wasn't quite deadly enough for our military anymore. Every now and then, someone would step outside the designated rally boundaries, and they would be tased and then cuffed. Later, they would be released with a fine and a warning. Mayor Randy told us again and again how he had made us safer.

◆ ◆ ◆

A mile away from my house, a SWAT team raided Ken M's house based on an anonymous tip. They fired tear gas into his home and crashed through the windows and abducted him. His young children were terrified. He spent three days in jail, but it turned out he'd done nothing wrong. He'd just made a teenager angry on the Internet; he'd gotten into a sports argument with a child and that child had tracked down his personal details and then called the police, saying he had credible evidence the man was a terrorist, stashing IEDs and other deadly weapons. The town paid to replace Ken's windows. Two weeks later, that same teenager called the SWAT team again and there was another standoff.

◆ ◆ ◆

Renee texted to say she had to see me, so I drove to her apartment. She poured us both tea, and then told me she had a confession: she'd been one of the tabloid leaks after my arrest.

"Okay," I said.

"This is when you're supposed to forgive me."

"I don't."

"To tell you the truth," Renee said, "when they showed that picture of you on the news, I wasn't surprised. I thought it could've been you." She leaned forward and blew on her tea. It was as if she were talking about the weather rather than telling me she thought I might be a mass murderer.

"It wasn't me."

"I know. I know," she said. "I'm just saying."

◆ ◆ ◆

I agreed to go shopping for fabrics with Renee. She was still one of the few people in Seldom Falls who wasn't afraid to be seen with me in public. Renee liked fabrics and yarns and glitters. She owned more varieties of candles than I'd ever seen. They were arranged in her house in such volume and with such precision that it looked like she was staging an occult ritual.

I don't know why she wanted me to go with her, because I'm not interested in crafting. Maybe she just felt safer with another woman by her side. Even before her divorce, she was anxious about being alone in public. As we walked down the yarn aisle, she told me about a recent assault on a woman. Most of Renee's information came from social media. "She was *with her kids*," she said. "Walking past a church. And some Mexicans just grabbed her and raped her in the back of a van and dropped her in a park." The villains in Renee's stories were generally Mexican. If there were any Mexicans in our town, I had never seen them. Everyone knew to be afraid, but didn't know whom to be afraid of. When the threat is ambiguous, you need to personalize it. It's not healthy to be afraid of the atmosphere itself, so you need to find the one who is poisoning it. Renee spent so much time being afraid of the strangers, but we all would have been much safer if we'd spent more time fearing the people who looked just like us. "Someone found her unconscious in the morning," Renee said. "And obviously her kids are traumatized forever." She picked up two balls of yarn, one red and one a little more red, and weighed them in her hands.

We entered an aisle full of dozens of types of feathers. Renee was somehow able to distinguish the different uses for each one. I was once told I was allergic to feathers, but I've never trusted doctors' diagnoses. Allergies are our way of rejecting nature.

Renee periodically scanned the store; I knew she was checking for emergency exits, because I was doing the same thing.

Our cart was filled with trinkets and baubles and so many different kinds of glitter. "Are we here for something specific?" I said.

"Would you rather be somewhere else?" She shook a bag of gemstones next to her ear like a maraca, listening for I don't know what. "Do you have something better to do?"

"Don't you?"

I made Renee stop at the liquor store on the way back to her house. She didn't drink anymore. She wasn't officially in any recovery program, but in her mid-twenties she woke up in a strange bed and had no idea how she'd gotten there. She'd blacked out half the weekends of her young adult life. She'd been robbed twice, men leaving with her purse while she slept off a dozen tequila shots. She was afraid of the person she used to be.

I poured Canadian Club into my tea. "Do you miss working?" I said. She had quit a few months ago and was trying to stretch her money out to live simply.

"Did you know forty percent of all deaths occur on the job?"

"That doesn't sound true."

"Have you looked it up? I've looked it up." She piled scrapbooking materials on her coffee table. "You can stay if you want, but I have work to do," she said. I refilled my mug.

I stayed at Renee's place for two days. She had plenty of food, her TV worked, and she had a high-speed Internet connection. We didn't talk much. When Robbie texted, I told him I needed a few days away. I didn't like feeling needed. I wanted nobody to want me for anything. Renee was busy cutting perfect circles and making precise folds in paper and then gluing things to other things. I was on her computer, searching for information on guns. *What is the best gun,* I searched. There was no clear answer. There are best guns for picking off varmints and best guns for home protection and best guns for stopping a black bear dead in its tracks and best guns for taking down enemy aircraft and best guns for enacting your childhood fantasies and best guns for getting the government off your back. I spent hours reading everything I could find.

Do I need a gun, I searched.

By the next morning, I'd received several emails advertising great deals on guns. Subject lines like:

Ensure Your Safety

Want to Be Safe?

A Dose of Sanity in an Insane World

Ads in the margins now promoted great deals:

Don't Forget the Ammo

The Most Powerful Weapon on the Market

On the morning of the second day, there was a box outside Renee's door, addressed to me. It contained fifty bullets. Free samples.

Feel the Power in Your Hands

I hadn't typed Renee's address anywhere. Someone knew what I was searching and where I was, and there was nothing I could do about it.

Pull the Trigger on Your Freedom

There was a flyer advertising a gun and knife expo.

Kill or Be Killed

It was all very simple. I could see the appeal.

Every time you type something, someone else can see it. Every thought you share with your computer is shared with the government, or with a hacker. They made computers indispensable, convinced us we all needed them to survive, and then after we bought them—and bought upgrades to them—they told us our computers were the most dangerous things in our homes. So they started monitoring us. It was for our own good. The only way to stay safe was to allow them in so they could see everything everyone was thinking at all times. Privacy is a commodity with so many conditions attached that your warranty is invalid by the time you open the box.

But the boy who did the shooting had a computer and they didn't find him. They didn't stop him.

So: they needed more access.

A congressman had proposed a bill allowing government agents to remotely access any computer on US soil without a search warrant. Random morality checks. If you're not a bad guy, then you don't have anything to worry about. All you're doing is sacrificing a little bit of privacy for the greater good.

• • •

I was not interested in being a good guy. I was even less interested in being a good girl. Good guys get to be aggressive. Good girls have to be quiet and submissive and do as they're told. Good guys get to be heroes. Good girls get to cook dinner for the heroes and wash their dishes afterward. Good guys get blowjobs, good girls give them. Good guys carry guns and feel safe and are surrounded by a force field of good-guyness. Good girls have to wait around for someone to save them.

• • •

On the walk home from Renee's house, a man in a suit and a $30 haircut approached me. He was wearing a wedding ring. He put his hand on my arm without my permission. He was bigger than me. He looked strong enough to jimmy open a window or kick down a dead-bolted door. He said, "I want you to know you are beautiful." When a man says a thing to you, you're supposed to smile and thank him for including you in his thoughts. It was morning and people were walking past us on their way to work. His hand was still on my arm. I felt like a fish flopping around on the deck of a boat, the fisherman deciding whether to keep me or throw me back. Deciding whether he should swing me around and crush my brains against the side of the boat so he could descale me and filet me and serve me inside a taco. He leaned down closer to me and said, "I want to make you an offer."

His breath smelled like old hot dogs. Like he'd eaten hot dogs for breakfast. Like he was a man who would eat hot dogs for breakfast and then grab the arms of women on the street. "I'll give you fifty bucks if you let me take a picture of you." I squirmed away. I hated that it could be described as squirming, that even my evasive tactics felt childish. "You don't have to get naked or anything. I just want to remember what you look like right now."

I shook my head. There were words I wanted to say, but they wouldn't line up in order in my mouth.

"Don't be such a bitch," he said, touching my arm again. Harder this time. "It's like an art thing. I'm not asking you to show me your tits."

Arms crossed over my chest, head down, I hustled away from him. Maybe people thought I was his wife and we were having a normal argument. Maybe they thought I was a prostitute. Maybe they didn't care.

If he wanted to, he could pick me up, throw me over his shoulder, and take me back to his house. He could lock me in his basement and chain me to the water heater.

"Fine. A hundred bucks," he said. "That's fair. You don't even have to *do* anything."

Everyone could use a hundred dollars. Between unemployment and my savings, I had about four months before I was in serious trouble. Letting a strange man take a clothed picture of me would take seconds and it would be easy. But then he would own my body. He would have it on his phone and carry me in his pocket. He would look at it whenever he was bored and I would have to appear in his mind and do terrible things with him. One day his wife would find pictures of me and dozens of other women in his phone. He would tell her he had to do things like this because she didn't do anything to make him feel sexy anymore. She would feel guilty.

I got to the intersection at Main and Magnolia. Rush-hour traffic sped by. He stood behind me, his hands on my hips like we were in the audience at a concert. "Last offer. Two fifty, but you have to take your shirt off." I felt his erection against my lower back. I swung my elbows wildly, and when he released his grip, I sprinted out into traffic. Part of me wanted to get hit. Part of me wanted him to see me broken and bleeding in the street and know it was his fault. Cars honked and I swerved and dodged and I kept running, and he stood on the other side of the street, yelling, "I didn't want to see your fat ass naked anyway."

◆ ◆ ◆

Women do not own their bodies. Men take pictures of us when we are not looking. They surreptitiously record videos of our legs on the bus and load them to the Internet, where other men can stare at our legs and masturbate. We wore a dress that day because it was hot outside, because it made us feel good about ourselves, because we had a date, because we felt entitled to dress however we liked. They gather in groups on corners and follow us home with their eyes. They leave the residue of their vision on our bodies. They tell us they love women because they love their mother and their sister and their daughter.

I should have taken the money. It would have been reparations for the way men have treated my body since I was thirteen, when my gym teacher, Mr. Gagne, called me into his office to tell me he could see my nipples through my shirt, and I should start wearing a bra or he might get the wrong message.

Every time a man meets a woman, he should have to give her $5. He should have to give her $5 and say, "I'm sorry." Then he should never talk again.

◆ ◆ ◆

One day late in August, a confession booth appeared on the corner near my favorite bar. Nobody knew who had put it there, but there were lines to get in. I went to the bar and sat where I could see through the window, waiting for someone to exit the booth. I would follow them home and see what they were doing with everyone's secrets. I staked the booth out every day for a week, twelve hours a day. I never saw anybody leave, not even to go to the bathroom. Finally, I decided to go myself. Nobody made eye contact while we waited in line. When it was my turn, I asked the person on the other side of the screen who she was, but she wouldn't tell me. She didn't say anything about Jesus or any other god. She said, "Tell me your sins." And I told her. I needed someone to know. I won't tell you what I confessed that time. That's between me and whatever god you believe in.

She listened and absolved me and told me to make my penance by calling my brother. I hadn't even told her I had a brother.

Before I'd learned of Calvin's existence, I'd felt I had a pretty good understanding of how things worked. I was never a happy child—my mother used to describe me as *somber*—but things made sense. After that morning when I found out about my brother, my vision doubled and cracked and doubled again. There is too much truth in the world for children to process. Adults should always lie to children. Children deserve the luxury of not really knowing their parents. They should only find out much later that they are the product of two foul-tempered and unreliable people who had no business running their own lives, let alone another's. My mother's spitefulness and my father's indifference and their casual cruelty to the brother I'd never even met were completely disorienting. I was knocked off my axis. In my dreams I saw my brother, the one I'd never met. I saw my father reaching into my chest like god yanking out Adam's rib, and creating this new person. I stopped sleeping. I avoided my parents during the day, and they made very little effort to find me. Their energy was devoted to hating each other. I created dozens of hiding spots around the house and in the yard. When I realized they didn't even notice my absence, I started stealing sips of my father's beer first to get in trouble and then, when still nobody noticed, to feel so imbalanced that the world made some kind of sense.

After Calvin was born, he and his mother were kicked out of their house. Her father, my father's friend, had disowned her and told her he would treat her as a trespasser if she ever came back. She spent the next few years staying with friends and getting arrested for taking recreational drugs. I was old enough to be aware of things like this, but not really to understand them. I had friends with older sisters who knew her and gossiped about her. One day, when I was twelve years old, she showed up at our door, with a suitcase and the boy who was my half-brother. I had never met him before, though sometimes my mother would slow the car down and point him out. I was the only one home when this girl knocked on my door. "This is Luther," she said. "He's going to stay here a while." I'd thought becoming a mother would turn someone old, but she still looked very young. I let him in and poured him a glass of milk. He didn't say anything. He wasn't crying, but he looked afraid. I tried to tell him jokes, but I didn't know what five-year-olds would find funny. I turned on the TV for him and then tried to figure out how to explain this to my mother when she came home. I thought she would throw both of us into the street. I thought she would fly into a rage so intense you could see it from space. Instead, when she opened the door and saw an abandoned boy she figured it out without asking any questions. She calmly collected his things and then lifted him up, carrying him upstairs to my bedroom. She'd shown him more love in the moment when she met him than she'd shown anyone in years. Later, she made him change his name. "Luther is not an appropriate name," she said, and she erased the past that had followed him through the door. It took him months to respond to Calvin, but soon we all forgot he'd ever had his name changed.

Calvin slept in my bed, and I was moved to a mattress on the floor. This was the arrangement until I moved to college. For the first two weeks, he cried. Children love their mothers even if their mothers don't love them. It's a structural defect. It's one of the best arguments against Intelligent Design. At night, while he cried in my bed, I would lie on the floor and tell him terrible things. I told him his mom had left him because he was a bad child. I told him we were going to cook and eat him. I told him there were bugs so small he couldn't even see them, and they were all over the walls, and at night they would crawl into his ears and lay eggs. I told him he was actually my pet, and I even put the leash on him one night. It was cruel. I was twelve and I'd lost my bed.

Two years later, his mother moved to another city and enrolled in high school as a junior under a fake name. They arrested her before she had a chance to graduate again. There was a time when it was possible to move away to a new city and assume a new identity and nobody would ever know. Now you're stuck with who you are. There are too many cameras. Everything you do is recorded. She started trying heavier drugs and all we know is she spent a few years alternating between rehab and jail. She got sober for a while and even got a job cleaning houses, but she eventually overdosed in the bathroom of a rich person's house. I found out when I saw my father crying in the dark after reading her obituary. I don't know when or how Calvin learned about it.

◆ ◆ ◆

I called my brother because I'd promised I would check in with him once a month, and I didn't want to risk him showing up at my front door if I waited any longer.

"Hey, big sister," he said. "I thought maybe you'd disappeared."

"I wouldn't even know how to disappear," I said.

In the background I heard his children screaming. I knew so little about them I couldn't even tell their screams apart. "If it's not a good time, I can call back later."

"They're just chasing the dog," he said. "Did I tell you we got a dog?"

I thought his wife was allergic to dogs. I asked him how things were. He told me about the dog, childhood milestones, a promotion at work. "Just look how fucking normal you are," I said. "Isn't it weird?"

"Normal is good. I like normal."

"Next time I call, you're going to be installing a picket fence and trying to sell me Girl Scout cookies." Normally our calls were a half hour long. I was nearly finished with my first glass of wine, so either this call had been going faster than I'd thought, or I was drinking too quickly.

He said something to his kids. I wasn't sure if he could even hear me over them. There was a brief debate on his end. I refilled my glass, knowing he could hear me opening the fridge and twisting the cap off the bottle. If he asked what I was doing, I would tell him I'd started drinking bottled water because of the lead in the public water. Or I would tell him I was getting ready to cook a meal. He'd always wanted to teach me how to cook, so he would like that lie. Harmless lies are the glue that keeps families together.

"Did you ever own a gun?" I said.

"I have two."

"Even with the kids there?"

"I got them for protection."

"Tell me I don't need a gun. Tell me it's a bad idea."

"Shit, Anna. It's a terrible idea."

• • •

When I was thirteen, I found an unloaded shotgun in my father's closet; I was too young to be afraid of it, so I dragged it out of the room, and my mother laughed. "What," she said to my father. "You're going to *kill* yourself now?" She took the gun away from me and tossed it to him. "Or you're going to kill me? Jesus Christ, Henry. Get a grip." He said nothing. She turned to me. "Your father has big ideas, but lacks conviction." He put the gun on the floor and went outside for a long walk.

. . .

Three airplanes had gone missing in one week. On TV, they guessed that the Russians were responsible, but the Russian president said nothing. The simplest explanation was that those planes had been destroyed because in some way their existence had inconvenienced a nation-state with too many missiles and not enough restraint. For a week, politicians in our country threatened war. But then nine people were killed in one night in Chicago, and six in St. Louis, and fourteen in Lansing. It was the middle of summer. People in the heart of the country were slaughtering one another. They said the heat made people more likely to kill. It was a good reminder of how simple we are as animals. When it's hot, we kill. When it's cold, we buy sweaters.

Every now and then someone from a forgotten country will plant a homemade bomb somewhere and remind everyone they exist. Most bombs are just the result of people trying to remind the world of their existence. Men do not have a language for loneliness, so they turn to violence and sports, in that order. They cannot cry, so they blow things up instead.

SEPTEMBER

OTHER SCHOOLS in the state had already begun classes, but our high school still hadn't reopened. A group of victims' parents said it should never open again but should instead stand as a memorial to those who had died. An activist group wanted it to be bulldozed and replaced with a memory garden. Renee thought the only way to heal would be to return the children to the school and proceed as normal. Robbie kept saying he wished everything could just be reset. Mayor Randy said it was important that we not give the shooter what he wanted. But he already had what he wanted. He already had our bodies and our minds. He already had his face on TV and his manifesto read by millions.

For a while, there had been nightly vigils. Parents and friends came to the school hoping to find answers to questions they never thought they'd ask. They'd hoped to see something they could never see again. But now we were being told to heal. We were being told that this must not define us.

In the interim, anyone could visit the site. People placed flowers and candles and other mementos in the grass next to the cafeteria. Teddy bears, weathered and filthy, sat heaped along the wall of the gym. Someone had spray-painted on the wall STILL WE SURVIVE.

Nobody had ever confiscated my keys when I was suspended, so one night, I let myself in and walked the ghost-filled halls. I can see ghosts because I nearly died once when I was seventeen and again when I was twenty. The first time, I flipped my mother's car speeding around a curve. A stranger pulled me out of the wreck, and I spent two weeks in the hospital. I needed months of physical therapy to learn how to walk normally again. The second time, I was thrown down a flight of stairs by a jealous college boyfriend. He said he didn't think I would actually fall, he was just trying to scare me. He was upset because I'd been talking to another guy in my class. He convinced me not to press charges because he was already on probation from some minor drug offenses, and one more strike would ruin his life. He said he was sorry. He said, "You just made me so *mad.*" When I tried to break up with him after that, he threatened to kill himself. We stayed together another six months. I only left him when he proposed to me and my survival instincts forced me to run.

Even before the shooting, there had been two ghosts in the school: the football player who suffered a freak injury on the field and died in the gym, and the geometry teacher who choked on an almond in front of his students. But now the halls were bustling.

Some of the bodies had lain there for two days during the

investigation. Professional cleaners had tried to buff the blood out of the floors, but if you looked you could still see the stains.

The first ghost I recognized was Todd F, the freshman boy who had become the face of the news coverage. He was tiny, so tiny it was hard to believe he was even in high school. His glasses were too big for his face. His backpack so overstuffed with books it looked like he was carrying an even tinier person on his back. They said Todd had been shot in the leg and was dragging himself along the hallway while the shooter followed and taunted him. Todd mumbled a prayer, and the shooter said, "I'm your god now!" They say Todd kept the shooter distracted while others ran to safety.

Todd's ghost did not look heroic. He looked like a boy running late for class. He paced between his locker and the old chem lab, which had been ravaged in the attack. Broken glass littered the floors, powerful solvents had spilled and eaten holes into desks. Bullet holes pocked the walls like acne scars. The teacher's desk was flipped on its side so students could shelter behind it. Todd passed through me, and my memory flashed to the moments just before the shooting, to Todd rushing out of the classroom, feeling sick and lonely, like he'd just somehow embarrassed himself in front of a group of girls. He was so wrapped up in his own teenage anxiety that he hadn't even noticed the alarms.

In my old classroom, my replacement's paperwork was still spread across the desk, ruined by the sprinklers that had been activated by the explosions. A couple windows were broken. But mostly it looked like my room. I imagined my room repopulated with surly boys in the back scribbling on the desktops, earnest boys in the front raising their hands, distracted and vain girls checking their reflections in their phones and waiting for someone online to validate them, nerdy girls embracing their unpopularity and trying to engage with the work, even a few boys craning their necks to try to see up my skirt as I sat on my desk with my legs crossed. I was doing my job and I was useful. Sometime in the future, when they were lamenting their lost youth, they would talk about my class. Some of them would remember how they'd been moved by a particular novel. They would laugh at the time I threw a copy of *Brave New World* at a sleeping boy's head. They would remember how much they hated my class and me and reading and words.

The day I was suspended, Hank T called me into his office and told me, "You are not an easy person to employ." I was in trouble because none of my students had done the assigned reading. I was in trouble because I'd told them that people who don't do the reading are statistically three times more likely to end up in jail, and when one of the boys rolled his eyes at me, I told him I wished his eyes would roll out the back of his head so I could stomp on them and grind them into the floor. And when he snickered at me with that disdainful teenage boy face of his, I took his bag from under his desk and threw it out the window. Hank T said things like this made me an unstable presence. A liability. He said, "I know you think the students love you, but they don't." I was too unpredictable, he said. If a teacher's biggest crime is being too interesting, then that teacher should be rewarded and not fired. There had been complaints, probably from students who had failed. Comments about how my grades were arbitrary and unfair. Suggestions that I'd picked on certain students and played favorites, but everyone has favorites. Neutrality and objectivity don't exist; some people are just afraid of owning their beliefs. There were questions about why some days we didn't have a plan—but not having a plan is a plan. Had no one ever watched a movie about a teacher? Had no one ever been *inspired* before? I figured out who some of the complainers were and I sent them messages online, but that only made things worse.

Hank asked me to leave, and I said I would, but that I deserved more warning than this. "You've gotten plenty of warnings," he said. I was being fired, though I didn't realize it until later.

On my way out, I kicked over his trash can and turned out the lights in his office. Someone keyed his car in the parking lot, and they blamed me for that too.

• • •

I needed to go out and see someone, so I called Robbie and then I called Renee and then I called Angie. None of them answered. When you need people, there are no people near you. When you don't need them, they surround you and smother you. I remembered being twelve years old and wanting urgently to get away from the little brother who had broken my family, and locking myself in my bedroom, but he sat on the other side of the door, crying, begging me to let him in. I left him out there for hours, trying to read a book, trying to just be a person by myself. When he stopped crying, I still saw his shadow under the door. I heard his sniffling breath. I felt his presence still crowding into my room, and soon my mother was banging on the door demanding I let him in, and then my father was there too, drill in hand. They removed my bedroom door and never replaced it. My father said I no longer deserved door privileges.

◆ ◆ ◆

When I was a teacher, I used to feel guilty about going to happy hour after work and then emerging, four drinks later, into a sun-lit afternoon while people in business clothes rushed home, and overachieving moms walked to the gym, and dads rode bikes down the street with their children. I used to worry that some parent would recognize me and I would have to explain my choice to be drunk midday. My justification then was that I had no responsibilities to tend to at home. But in small towns people get reputations, and I did not want a reputation.

Now, with the sun gone and our circadian rhythms disrupted, nobody judged you for ordering a shot and a beer at noon on a Monday.

My favorite bar, across the street from the confession booth, was called Murphy's Law. It was owned by a retired cop named Murphy, who had heard the phrase but didn't know what it meant. It was a half mile from the school. It used to be a mile away but the gravitational pull of the mass murder had drawn everything closer to the hub; everything in town had contracted and tightened like atoms in winter.

The sandwich-board sign on the sidewalk said THE PLACE

WHERE GOOD FRIENDS MEET. I needed a good friend, and I went there most days ready to meet one.

◆ ◆ ◆

As a teenager, I had four good friends. We dressed alike and we made one another laugh and we spent afternoons drawing pictures of our teachers doing terrible things to one another in the lounge. We discussed strategies for meeting boys and what to do with them if we were alone, how to avoid getting pregnant. We watched movies about women falling in love with men who refused to take no for an answer. We listened to music and danced. We smoked pot and lied to one another. We talked about all the things we hated about ourselves, our faces and our arms and our hair and our butts and our personalities. One of those girls is dead; she was stabbed by an ex-boyfriend who'd been stalking her. The second friend still lives in Seldom Falls but we haven't spoken in over a decade; when we see each other in public, we don't even say hello anymore. The third friend works for a company in Seattle that sells cute magnets with pithy sayings on them, about weight loss and about Mondays being a particularly bad day of the week. The last one moved away to college and disappeared so completely from my life that I've sometimes wondered whether she even existed at all.

◆ ◆ ◆

Most of the regulars at Murphy's Law had lived in this town their whole lives and had lost their jobs in the recession. Seldom Falls had once been one of the country's leading manufacturers of elevator parts. We had a massive factory by the lake. Everybody worked there, building buttons, pulleys, gears. But factories die, and nobody realized this, and there is no such thing as reincarnation. There was no compelling reason for Seldom Falls to continue existing except that it was already full of people. And so everyone got a little shabbier each year. They grew up in one world and then found themselves suddenly dying in another. The man next to me was overweight and the way he groaned when he sat, it sounded like he'd been walking for days. His name was Brady. He had worked at least a dozen different jobs around town, and had always been friendly enough to me. If you live in a place like Seldom Falls long enough, you recognize everyone. It allows you to trick yourself into believing you really know them. Brady had a beard so thick it looked like there might not even be skin beneath it, like if he shaved there would just be no face at all. His lips were the color of Mountain Dew, and his hands shook as he waited for his first drink.

He knew who I was but was polite enough not to mention it. He was here like I was because there was no compelling reason to be somewhere else. The TVs above the bar were tuned to the news with the sound off and the captions on.

He looked like he needed a good friend.

"You ever think there's too many bones?" Brady said. "We have two hundred and six bones. That's way too many things to break."

I hadn't thought of it, but he was right.

"I know you need your bones," he said. "Don't get me wrong.

I thank the good lord for all the bones I do have. It's just. Why not a few less?"

"I broke my femur once," I told him. That wasn't true; I had broken bones before, but never that one. It just seemed like the most dramatic bone to break.

"Shit. Shit shit shit." He motioned to the bartender for a refill. "How old were you?"

"Sixteen."

"What kind of fucking world is it where sixteen-year-olds can break their fucking femurs? You have to go to rehab?"

I told him I did. I told him it had been grueling.

He buried his face in his hands.

I stood to reassure him that I was fine now. I did a little hip-shaking dance move. I decided not to tell him that when I was sixteen a boy in my high school pinned me against my locker and reached up my skirt and forced his fingers inside me while his friends watched and called me a slut. I didn't think he would be able to handle that.

He clinked his glass against mine. He was in the habit of glass clinking as a sort of punctuation. "Here's to working femurs," he said.

"Here's to being able to run away," I replied.

All the seats in the bar had filled. The jukebox played songs about the South and songs about guitars and songs about sex. On the news they were talking about a celebrity whose nude pictures had been stolen from her phone. The scrolling ticker said most of the world's polar bears were dead. It said someone in Atlanta had shot nine people at a carnival.

I was out of money, but Brady said he'd cover me. It was possible I was permanently out of money. I didn't know. They wouldn't accept my card. I was supposed to be applying for jobs.

"One thing they don't talk about on the news," Brady said, "is the gangs."

I said I supposed he was right again, though it seemed to me that some days all they talked about on TV was gangs. Why else would I know the names of the major street gangs in Chicago? Why else would I know what MS-13 was? There was profit in convincing us that gangs ran the cities and soon they would be here. The farther away you move from the rest of the world, the more paranoid you are about them eventually catching up to you.

"The gangs, when you get in their way, you know what they do? They don't kill you. They cut off your tongue to send a message. Or they cut off your balls and nail them to your front door."

I was happy, I said, not to have balls then. I asked him how he'd learned so much about gangs, and he said he'd watched a couple specials on TV.

"I don't think I've ever seen a gang," I said.

"Well, they're not here yet." In the papers they were saying crime was actually down across the country, but Brady said that was a lie; it was just to keep people from panicking.

I told him I'd been thinking about a bomb shelter.

"You think a gang can't get inside a bomb shelter?" he said. "Gangs do whatever they want."

"So what are you going to do?"

He chugged half a pint. "With any luck, I'll be dead long before they show up," he said.

A man had been eavesdropping on our conversation. He shared his own theories about creeping death. He said things were much different when he was a kid. He said he couldn't believe what had happened to his country. "We used to not even lock our doors," he said.

We used to not even lock our doors. People always said this. The world wasn't safe when we were young, but it felt safe. Maybe we should have been locking doors. I remember being young and wishing I could lock my door. I remember not even having a door.

• • •

When I got home from the bar, I found an envelope from Calvin. He'd written a short note saying he was thinking about me. Harlan had drawn a series of scribbles and circles meant to represent me and him standing under the sun. Children love people because they're told to love them and they don't know how to do anything else. They draw pictures for adults because it's all they have to offer.

VICTIMS, PART II

KARINA R TRANSFERRED to our school in sixth grade. Her family had recently moved from Warsaw, and though she spoke excellent English, she was bullied mercilessly for her accent. She sat next to me in classes and got in the habit of writing notes to me on her own legs. She would hike her skirt up and write on her thigh in marker: *I hate this place*. At first, I thought the notes were private, like a living diary. One day she wrote *Everybody here is ugly*—and handed me the marker and presented her thigh to me. *They're dumb too*, I wrote, and she laughed.

For the next two months, we covered each other's skin in notes, first surreptitiously in class, and later in her bedroom, writing up and down each other's arms and legs and bellies. The marker says it's permanent, but if you scrub hard enough, it goes away, and so we felt free to expose the darkest thoughts we had, before washing them off and starting over the next day. It was the most intimate experience of my life. But soon she became popular because she would steal vodka from her parents and get drunk with the boys in the woods, and then she got a sixteen-year-old boyfriend. By the end of the year, she'd begun spreading rumors that I was a lesbian. If we'd been boys, I would have just fought her. Instead I internalized all the hatred and scorn and let it fester.

Karina moved away years ago, but her younger brother still lived here and was working maintenance at the school when the shooter arrived. He was wounded, losing the use of his right arm. I wanted to visit him in the hospital and leave a note on his arm while he slept, but I was afraid people would see me.

◆ ◆ ◆

Kelsey P was a mediocre student but a pretty good artist, who I always figured would end up in advertising someday, living in New York City and saying things like, "I cannot *believe* I used to live in a place where you can't get Thai food after midnight." The first bullet entered through her right eye and the second bullet ripped through her lung. They said she might survive, but they didn't know what kind of life she might live.

◆ ◆ ◆

Sue G lived four houses away and only came outside occasionally to yell at the neighborhood children to stop touching her fence—it was a white vinyl fence and it had cost her a lot of money, she said, and when they laughed at her she lectured them about the rising costs of oil, and if anyone really pushed her, she started on her problems with the Arabs. She had lived there as long as I could remember, since I was a teenager at least. "You think I don't know your parents?" she yelled, point-lessly. "You think I don't know everybody?" Just the act of know-ing people was a threat. She had collected secrets.

Every afternoon there were more packages on her doorstep. Sometimes they got delivered to me by accident. Sometimes I opened them. Often, they were fish-tank accessories, or fish-related products, like a pillow that looked like a trout or a wall sign that featured a bass saying *Who you callin' Big Mouth?*

Some people like fish.

I sometimes delivered them to her door and pretended the box had been sliced open before I received it. She never invited me in, but peering over her shoulder, I saw junk piled up to the ceilings; she'd had to carve a path through the piles just to navigate her own house. It smelled terrible, like the sawdust a school janitor throws on a puddle of vomit. It was like her house was slowly digesting her. Her son, Michael, was a cop, the kind of casually corrupt one who would demand free food at the deli and flash his lights just to blow through stop signs. He was on the scene at the school, and he took two bullets to the leg, but he would survive. He would have to retire from the force and live on disability in his mother's garbage-filled house. After he moved in, I heard her screaming at him many nights as he dragged lumpy black bags out to the curb; overnight she sneaked out and ran-sacked her own trash.

• • •

Alex A was wise beyond his years, but only by a few days. He spent most of his time hanging around the movie theater, drinking vodka and Sprite from a large soda cup. He was twenty when he finally graduated from high school, and years later most of his friends were still high school students. He had a steady supply of pot and a small apartment where they could listen to psychedelic rock and hide from their parents. When I was fifteen, I had a twenty-nine-year-old boyfriend named Miles, who was just like Alex. We sat in his sad apartment while he spun records and lectured me on music history, telling me why this band or that band is particularly important. Sometimes I brought Calvin with me, and Miles kept him entertained with video games and candy. I'd sworn Calvin to secrecy about what happened in that apartment. Miles taught me how to roll joints and he drove me places when I wanted to be driven to places. I felt very mature. We had aggressively mediocre sex, though I didn't realize at the time it could be better than that. Whenever I saw Alex A standing outside McDonald's with a high school girl staring up at him as if he were so wise, I was embarrassed to feel a pang of wistfulness. I don't miss being a teenager, but I miss that naïve feeling of having discovered something the rest of the world is too dumb to have figured out. Alex was there on the day of the shooting, working for a plumber called in to repair a leaking toilet. For two months, his post outside the theater was abandoned, and then one day he was there again, leaning on a cane, his right leg heavily bandaged, a divot in his head where he'd lost some of the bone.

• • •

Lily F's father had once won a morning radio contest by eating one of the host's toenail clippings on the air. He'd done this to earn a $25 gift card and a life-size replica of a famous cartoon panda, posed in the midst of a jump kick. The replica was placed in the center of the family's front lawn. Lily F's father spent his evenings cleaning it, decorating it for upcoming holidays: a party hat for New Year's, bunny ears for Easter, beads for Mardi Gras. I'd heard from a neighbor that his wife hated that he devoted so much energy to maintaining a movie prop, but it was a strange bit of whimsy I enjoyed. It made me feel like I was living in a place with interesting people. After the shooting, he dressed the panda in a black kimono and surrounded it with photos of his daughter. The panda has been in mourning ever since.

• • •

Kareem D had a mother who was friendly, but unstable. Everyone in town recognized her. When I was a teenager, before Kareem was ever born, I saw her walking all over Seldom Falls, sometimes ten miles in a day. She was a decade older than me, but looked three times that. One of her legs was slightly shorter than the other, so her stride was lopsided but surprisingly fast. She always carried a tote bag over her right shoulder. Later, I learned that she sometimes found stray animals and put them in the bag to carry them to shelters.

She covered so much ground, I thought she might be a ghost. When I was seventeen, my parents took me and my brother to an orchard thirty miles outside town—it was meant to be a bonding experience, an all-American apple-picking event—and while my parents bickered afterward about what we were going to do with fifteen pounds of apples, I swear I saw her, Kareem's eventual mother, looking into her bag and talking to something. An hour later, pulling into our driveway, my parents still fighting, I saw her again at the top of our street. It would have been impossible for her to have beaten us back there on foot. My mother went inside and spent the evening baking pies. My father ate them out of spite until he got sick. I was made to deliver the remainder to neighbors.

This was not long before Kareem's mother got pregnant. Even during the pregnancy she walked, and for a while, people around town hoped that having a child would be good for her. She went missing sometimes, hospitalized for one reason or another, and Kareem lived with his father. I hadn't even thought about her in years until I saw Kareem's face on the news. He was a high school senior, but I remembered his sad, precocious eyes. I remembered seeing him once walking alongside his mother for who knows how long, his own bag over his shoulder, and the two of them talking as if everything were normal and would be just fine.

OCTOBER

MET ANGIE SPARKS at the New Faith Bible Church. I'd called her to say I was interested in giving salvation a shot, and she invited me to join her for a service.

Angie gave me another pamphlet. This one was also about how the world was going to end. After you find God, he gives you a box full of pamphlets and the rest is up to you.

The reverend hugged me. His name was Chet. His skin felt like old newspapers. Later, I learned he had sworn off drinking water because he thought it would bring him closer to God. In his vestments, he looked like a haggard crow. He looked like a bird pretending to be a man.

"Tell me about the end of the world," I said.

Angie told me about her visions. When she prayed in her home, she concentrated very deeply until she saw images of the future. She knew how all of her acquaintances would die. Most people die unremarkably. An organ stops working. A stranger's car makes a left turn against a red light. We run out of oxygen. A tumor drains our life away. "You'll be the first of us to go," Angie said. "I'm sorry to tell you. I've seen it so many times now. Satan's army arrives on Earth and you're standing right there in front of them, and they just trample you. You get trampled." She held my hand like a doctor delivering news of terminal cancer. God knows exactly what's going to happen, and sometimes he slips hints to the prophets, but it's impossible to distinguish between prophets and madmen.

There were twenty other people in the room. They were mostly white and mostly men and mostly poor, though most people I knew were poor. The other church members' clothes didn't fit quite right. Their skin didn't fit quite right. We sat in a circle and Reverend Chet led us in prayer. He told us about the apocalypse, about the horsemen and the dragons and the lake of fire. When the world ends, we become collateral damage, incinerated in the crossfire between the archangels and hell's minions. When Chet spoke about the apocalypse, his face turned red and sweaty. He vibrated with anticipation. He jumped out of his seat and paced laps around us. He turned his back and shouted up at the ceiling. "I don't like having all this knowledge," he said. "I'd like to be like you were, like all those people out there. To go home and watch TV and not even think about the end of the world. To listen to pop music and eat candy all night long. To pet dogs and cats. To go outside without seeing the signs everywhere, without feeling the clammy handshake of demons, without seeing the faces of God's fallen angels on our street corners. But this is my curse, and my mission." He fell to his knees and crawled to me, grabbing my hand. "I know you can feel it too. You see that

the sun is gone. You feel the cold. How much longer can we survive in a world like this?" Every day it got colder. Even indoors,
we all wore our jackets. "I need you to place your hand on my
head right now and feel the knowledge radiating from me. I want
to transfer it to you," he said, and I did, and I waited to feel it. He
strained and pushed and I waited. "Do you *feel it*?" he shouted,
again and again until I pulled my hand back as if I'd just touched
a hot stove. I said I'd felt it. I wanted to have felt it. To tell you the
truth, I was hoping he'd have a more unique vision. Horsemen
and fire and everything else had been done before. If I could give
notes to him I'd tell him: punch it up a little. Surprise the people.

He kissed me on the mouth and then spun away, continuing
his sermon. He asked Jesus to come back to Earth and free us
all from the shackles of our imperfect bodies. He said we were
God's warriors preparing to fight in the battle against evil. He
said we were willing to do anything to bring about God's king-
dom on Earth. I bowed my head and mouthed my amens at
the appropriate times. I pictured myself in my heavenly armor,
with my heavenly spear. I pictured the devils with their hellish
armor and hellish spears. I imagined being devoured by a fiery
hellhound, its fangs plunging into my deep tissue and filling me
with venom. I thought maybe it would be easiest if I just found a
good hiding place and rode out the storm. When the end times
come, you have to pick a side, but there's no way of knowing
who's going to win.

After the prayer session, there was more prayer. Each person was asked to say some things about God, and describe their
personal struggle. The first man said he'd spent the whole week

banging on doors and warning people. He was arrested once for being too aggressive in delivering the good news. The police these days had little tolerance for unexplained aggression. He also mentioned that his water heater was on the fritz, which had been a real hindrance, shower-wise. "You go door-to-door looking like the smelly hobo guy and people don't listen to you," he said. The next man had been recently fired. He described his boss as a godless bitch who couldn't deal with him spreading the truth about our crumbling world. He wanted to get revenge on her first, then he would repent.

When it was my turn to pray, I told them all I wanted was to know how to feel safe again. I said I wasn't sure who was even in the government, let alone how they were supposed to help me. I said I was going to buy a telescope so I could find a planet more hospitable to human life. I didn't know when I was supposed to stop talking, or how to signal I was done. I made the sign of the cross and then sat down.

◆ ◆ ◆

My mother was a difficult woman to love. It was unclear whether she even wanted to be loved. When I was thirteen, she bought a deli, even though she'd never owned a business in her life. It was her favorite deli when she was growing up. The owners had no heirs and were retiring, so my mother bought the place on the spot. The meager price cleaned out her savings and she didn't consult with my father. One day she went out for sandwiches and came home with a deed. She had memories of her father lifting her up to the counter so she could eat samples of cheese, and she wanted to buy those memories back. During the next four years, we rarely saw her, because she was out the door by sunrise and home long after the dinner rush. My mother was a whisper and my father was a phantom; he was there but you could see through him. I took care of my brother, whom I had begun learning to love, and tried to wish myself into a different life. At the end of the day my mother would come home and open a bottle of Moscato and sit on the end of the couch swirling the wine in her mouth, coating her tongue in the sticky sweetness. She made sounds like a purring cat and said, "Momma earned you today," and then she poured herself another glass. Soon she asked me to just bring the bottle to her and then she grabbed my face with her hands and studied my eyes. She asked if I was smoking marijuana and laughed at me when I said no. Then she leaned in and kissed me on the forehead. Her hands smelled like raw onions and her breath like wine, and still that smell is the first thing I remember when I think of her.

During that same winter, my father lost his job again. He'd been laid off ten years earlier and had spent most of my life stringing together one bad job after another. After being fired this time, he went out with the boys from work and while we were eating dinner he came trundling through the door, his pockets stuffed with loose cigarettes he'd won in a low-stakes poker game. He took a plate of food and carried it to the couch, where he ate by himself. My mother did not even acknowledge he existed. She said nothing, to anyone, until after I put my brother to bed and then pretended to sleep myself. I sneaked out of my room to listen, sure they would have a terrible fight. He was on the couch, barely conscious from the booze. She sat next to him and said, very calmly: "I will not allow you to turn my life into a cliché." She left him there, and I heard him crying. Later, my father told me she'd held a knife to his throat when she said it. He was never an honest man, but I always believed him more than anyone else.

In our family we didn't talk about love. When I was young, if I told my mother I loved her, she would nod and say, "That's nice." Sometimes she would say, "You know how I feel about you." Love is an illness. Thinking in terms of love and not-love is a mistake. The questions to ask yourself are: do these people make me feel better or worse? How much are these people going to hurt me, and how much can I hurt them back?

We were raised to believe in the inherent goodness of the place where we lived, but Seldom Falls was never a great place. It was always just a place. My brother lost his faith in it before I did. He always knew how ugly places can be when people think they're safe. The media reminded us constantly that safe, happy places aren't actually safe or happy so much as they're deluded into believing they are. But it's such a comforting delusion, to think that if you retreat to the right city, then suddenly you're free of all the dangers. You can build a fort with twenty-foot-high walls, but you can't keep the wilderness out.

◆ ◆ ◆

I brought Robbie with me to the gun expo at the East Township Convention Center because we needed to get out of the house, and because Reverend Chet had asked me to acquire some weapons for the church. They were stockpiling an arsenal. Neither of us had ever fired a real gun. Robbie played paintball on weekends, and as a teenager had made some extra cash playing semiprofessionally. He enjoyed the thrill of the chase, the opportunity to playact murdering his friends. He enjoyed being shot and surviving. There was enough weaponry in the East Township Convention Center to eradicate the species of your choice. It took God forty days and forty nights to wipe the Earth clean of almost everyone, but it would take Robbie and me only a few hours if we set our minds to it. There were so many vendors, it was impossible to know where to begin. At least twenty rows of tables, all with their own colorful displays and patterned tablecloths and stacks of paperwork and groggy salesmen nursing coffee and checking their phones every couple minutes. If not for the hundreds of men fondling guns, it would have looked exactly like any other convention.

The first table we passed was selling a new scope that allowed shooters to magnify potential targets from a hundred feet farther away than ever before. A poster showed a before-and-after image, first of an empty field and then a close-up of an oblivious deer's face. Presumably that particular deer hadn't been shot after the photo was taken, and he never knew how close he'd come to being killed for sport. He just munched on grass and looked for doe and then rubbed his antlers on a tree. He trotted into the woods and later lay down safely at night and never knew that he was one twitch of an index finger away from having had a bullet implanted in his brain, his skin removed and turned into wallets, his meat stripped away from the bone and salted and dried and turned into jerky, his head sawed off and mounted on a piece of wood and then hung on display in someone's sitting room. The scope seemed like a very good tool for someone who wanted to kill from very far away.

I was sure the FBI was still watching me. I knew there would be undercover agents at the gun expo, dressed in John Deere hats and ill-fitting jeans. I was one of probably a hundred people in the room being monitored for potential activities deemed dangerous to the state. There is no such thing as being removed from the threat list. You can get downgraded, but you're still in the system.

Many booths displayed signs that said ARE YOU PREPARED? I was not prepared. That was the whole problem.

Their pamphlets and videos told stories of terrified women enduring home invasions. Of being tied up and gagged and feeling powerless while the invader ransacked their house and made off with family heirlooms. Of being sexually assaulted and left for dead. "All across the country," the narrator of one video said, "innocent families are in danger." They showed a montage of potential perpetrators: drug addicts, illegal immigrants, perverts, terrorists, sociopaths. "This country is in crisis," the narrator said. "There's only one way to ensure your safety."

The men in this room were prepared with every kind of survival tool imaginable. Traps to arrange on your lawn. Tactical pants with built-in tourniquets in case you sustain a serious leg wound. Kits for making decoy versions of yourself, so you could get the drop on invaders. They were like Boy Scouts, but with more weapons.

By the end of our walk through the first row, I could barely breathe. The people in this room were invested in creating a mania of fear, and then promising they had the solution. What would I do if someone broke in? What would Robbie do? A kitchen knife is no defense against a criminal with a handgun. You needed to be better equipped than the criminals. You needed to stop thinking of guns as guns and start thinking of them as a home defense system. I told Robbie I had to leave. Just being in the room filled me with a dread I didn't think I could ever forget. We didn't buy any guns. The thought of exchanging money for a gun made me want to drive my car off the road and into the lake. If I were alone with a gun, I don't know what would happen. The gun would talk to me, and I would not know how to respond, and it would tell me things, and I would believe them all. I would do whatever it told me to do.

• • •

At Robbie's apartment, we pulled the cushions off the couch and flipped it on its side, then draped a sheet over it like a roof. We sat in our shelter and ate beans out of a can and drank half a bottle of cognac. We discussed what we would miss most about the outside world. Robbie said he would miss birds. My answer was traffic lights, seeing them change from green to red and back again. They made so much sense.

Sometimes with Robbie I would find myself having a pleasant conversation and then feeling suddenly overwhelmed by the urge to hit him, to destroy something in his face. I don't know why. He was not a man who deserved to have his face destroyed, and yet, the feeling would creep up in me, like a need to vomit. Sitting in the bomb shelter, I had to focus all my energy on suppressing the urge to shatter Robbie. In these moments, in the desire for senseless violence and the promise of relief at the sight of someone else in pain, I never felt more masculine. But violence doesn't cure violence; it creates violence. If I hit him, he would hit me back. And then I would hit him again, and eventually one of us would have to kill the other.

• • •

The shooter owned many video games, and he listened to a very aggressive genre of music. It became conventional wisdom to blame his preferred entertainments for the mass murder. A group of concerned parents gathered at the center of town to hold a bonfire. Parents were encouraged to bring questionable entertainments and throw them into the fire. It would be a mass exorcism.

The event was held at the clock tower on Main Street. When I was teenager, Seldom Falls had built the clock tower in an effort to help revitalize downtown, but nobody goes downtown to see a clock. There was a period in human history when not knowing the time was normal. There was a time when all the news you heard came from your neighbors, and the only things you knew about the rest of the world came from books.

Since the sun's disappearance, the cold had settled so deeply into my bones that I had forgotten what it was like to be warm. I didn't shiver anymore; I just felt a coldness like the heart of a crocodile. I felt myself some nights turning into a crocodile, scales forming on my skin, my eyes going glassy and my teeth clenching in a malevolent grin. I felt a strong desire to submerge myself in a lagoon and linger motionless, only my eyes peeking above the surface, while I waited for my prey to swim directly into my mouth.

I went to the bonfire because I was tired of the cold. The city council had called on the governor to officially declare a state of emergency. Even though they had installed powerful lights and heat lamps everywhere, they couldn't replace the sun. Six months of sunlessness had ruined all the crops. People had never quite adjusted. We were maladjusted. The steady darkness interspersed with occasional cones of artificial light was disorienting. Other cities still had a sun. I'd seen it; I took a bus across state lines just to confirm, and there it was. There were people in bathing suits at poolside and people with sunburns and people sweating through their shirts. How could the sun leave one place but not another?

On the stage behind the bonfire pit a woman yelled into a megaphone: "We must end violence today!" and people cheered. I cheered too. "Where does violence come from?" she said, and some people shouted answers even though it was clearly a rhetorical device. "It comes from giant corporations feeding our children slop. From video games that teach us not to value human life. Movies about zombies and TV shows about serial killers. Music with coded messages teaching kids how to kill." She bent down to a pile at her feet and grabbed a handful of video games. "My own son went to that school. It could have been him who was killed. It could have been him who turned out to be the killer." She tossed the games into the fire pit while a pair of men sprayed lighter fluid on it. "We need to reject these evil entertainments and purify ourselves," she shouted.

The fire started slowly and then suddenly roared upward as people tossed more and more garbage into it. The smoke was black and acrid. Nobody had anticipated the toxic smell of hundreds of pounds of burning plastic. Even breathing the air around the fire felt dangerous. Arms of flame leaped out of the pile as if trying to grab the nearest bystander. I kept getting closer. I wanted to sweat. I wanted to break the fever of the past few months. I stood so close to the fire I felt like I was inside it. The fire was the first thing I'd felt in weeks that wasn't false. It was real and simple and it could have killed me if an officer hadn't shoved me backward.

◆ ◆ ◆

Each time there was another shooting, they told us the cause was a mystery and there was nothing we could have done about it, except pray that it didn't happen again. To say something if we saw something. On the morning news, they discussed what to do if you found yourself in an active shooter situation. The best thing to do was not to shelter in place, as they used to teach, but to run to the nearest exit. "Put as much distance between yourself and the bullets as possible," the detective on TV said. "If there are bodies, step over them. Do not tend to the bodies." Leave the bodies behind. Use the bodies as a shield if it comes to that.

Seven dead in a mall in the Ann Arbor suburbs. One dead, thirteen wounded at a high school in Oakland. Four dead, two critical at a Little League baseball game in Tallahassee. Five dead outside an elementary school in Greensboro. Fifteen shot— the newspaper said "sprayed by bullets" which made it sound almost nice—by an assault rifle at a political rally in Tempe. Before the blood dries and clots, there's another one to report. Somewhere right now there is a boy acquiring a gun. There is a boy writing a manifesto. There is a man, angry at having been forgotten, at having been passed over, at finding out what life really is, loading his gun. There is a man fortifying his home and preparing for war. Listen and you can hear the hammers being cocked.

Because people kept getting murdered in places where murder isn't supposed to happen, the president announced he was going to take a tour of the massacre sites. He said, "This wave of violence is a great shame in the history of our great nation," and he pledged to keep us safe. He never said the word "gun." He never said the word "murder." He kept saying "tragedy." It was as if he were talking about the weather. He spoke of the virtues of small-town America. The politicians loved small towns. They thought all we did was sit around eating apple pie and waving flags in our churches. They didn't like to think about everyone taking opiates and working bad jobs and living in a constant state of fear. Their love for Main Street, USA, was malignant. We were dying and they were getting rich off of it while they praised us for our resilience. They stopped to have a beer with a local. They ate something deep-fried. They promised that next time they came through, they would bring prosperity with them. The president would be in Seldom Falls in six weeks.

◆ ◆ ◆

Another envelope from Calvin arrived. This time it contained a check. I don't know how he had money to spare. I also didn't know how I was going to continue paying my bills without his help. The destructive part of my brain told me to tear it up and toss it into the wind. I hated the thought of my younger brother having to take care of me. I didn't know how to take care of myself. I kept the check. I texted him. I said, "No more charity."

NOVEMBER

ROBBIE WAS CONCERNED about my mental state. He said, "Babe, I'm concerned about your mental state." He put his hand on my face and made me look at him—it was one of the most sincere gestures he'd ever made. I wished he weren't wearing a backward hat when he did it. I wished he looked more like someone's father, with gray hair around his temples and gray eyes haunted by the war and a mouth like a tightrope stretched between the towers of his cheekbones. I wanted him to be my father, with his cold hands and his broken tooth and his Michelob breath and his distant, useless love.

I grabbed the remote and turned on the TV. He took it from me and turned it back off.

"You have to do something about it," he said. "You are not healthy."

Isn't everyone unhealthy? Health is a condition of being between unhealthful periods. I told him I would get better. It just needed time.

"You can't just wait for things to get better."

He wanted me to see a therapist. Get some meds. Start keeping a diary. I told him I would think about it. But what would I get from a psychiatrist besides more judgment? Why did I need another person to perform for, another person to tell me what I was doing wrong? Now Robbie wanted me to spend time sitting in an office doing what? Talking about myself? Trying to open up my brain and hoping it didn't spill all over the floor?

It's not as if I'd never been to therapy before. When I was a freshman, my teachers accused me of acting up in class. They said I'd become a troublemaker. Outbursts and failures of decorum. "It's just hormones," my father said. The principal scheduled a weekly appointment with the school therapist; I would be held back a grade if I didn't comply. The therapist was a man in his late twenties who spent most of his time telling me this was not the job he'd signed up for. "I didn't go to school for eight years so I could help little girls get over their breakups," he said. Our meetings lasted only a half hour, and every week I told him I just wanted to be angry for a while, but I would be better soon. He made me keep an anger journal, but never checked it. Sometimes he talked about his girlfriend, who was pressuring him to buy her an engagement ring. "What's the fucking rush with women anyway? Have you ever even met a happy married person?" he said. I told him I had not. "Something happens to women when they get to their twenties," he said. "They change. They go from being fun and open-minded to being some other thing. They turn miserable." I sat quietly, waiting until I was given permission to leave. "My advice to you is to enjoy the age you are now instead of always being mad about it. Girls your age are perfect, and they don't even know it." He started showing up late for our meetings, and a month later, he was gone. They said he just left town one night without telling anyone.

◆ ◆ ◆

Robbie started leaving the phone numbers for therapists on the coffee table, and when that didn't work, he markered a number on my hand while I slept, and when that didn't work he went ahead and called someone nearby to make an appointment. When they called to confirm, I canceled. I told them they had the wrong number. I told them Anna Crawford had died years ago.

In the time I'd known Robbie, I had never seen him yell. When he got angry he would sulk and stop talking and pick at his toenails. He would be unresponsive for a few hours and eventually talk to me about something else. But when I told him I'd canceled the appointment, he yelled. He smashed my phone on the floor. He held my face in both of his hands and he leaned in to direct the words straight into my brain and he said, "You are not allowed to be like this anymore." He said, "You are letting this thing turn you into a terrible person." He pushed me and I stumbled backward, falling into the wall. His face had transformed into something dangerous. It was the face of a man who wanted to pummel the sadness out of me. He stared at me for a while and I wanted to stare back but I was afraid. If he wanted to, he could punch right through my face and shatter all the little bones. He yelled a profanity and then kicked the coffee table several times. He limped out of the room.

I compromised. I consulted a therapist online. She interacted with me through a chat bubble. She sent me links to helpful resources and said things like "How are you feeling today?" Like "We can talk about whatever you want to talk about" and "Your reaction is totally reasonable." She was using a script, but it was a good script. We talked a lot about post-traumatic stress disorder. We talked about how it manifests, the way it causes people to live in denial of their pain, to suffer occasional horrifying flashbacks, to feel guilt for having survived a trauma. When she logged off, she said, "I know you're going to be okay." She didn't know that, but it was a nice thing to say.

• • •

I read a book once about a man who'd lost the capacity for memory, who every morning started with a blank slate. The book treated it as a tragedy, and the character eventually had some sort of surgery to try to correct it, but the condition struck me as a blessing. The deepest miseries come from our capacity for remembering; if everything can be wiped away with a single swipe, then nothing has to hurt. We never have to know whom we've wronged, who has wronged us, who should be there but is no longer there.

• • •

Before April, if you had asked me to pick someone in town who would have been responsible for a mass shooting, I would have picked Skip G. I met him years ago when he worked at the pet store, during my ill-fated effort at owning a cat. Skip worked the register and he seemed very knowledgeable about pet supplies. He told me he'd sampled every food in the place, because if it's good enough for his babies, then it should be good enough for him. I asked him many questions because I'd never owned a pet before. He thought I was flirting. If you smile more than once at a man, he assumes you are in love with him. Eventually, I agreed to a date; it was the least I could do. Our date began with cheeseburgers and beers and ended at his apartment, where he introduced me to his babies. In three different glass aquariums, he kept three constrictor snakes. They had names: Zeus and Kong and Larry, who was named after one of the Three Stooges. He asked if I wanted to hold one. I did not want to hold a snake, and yet, even as I was responding, he was placing Larry on my shoulders. Its oily weight made my legs buckle. Snakes are a single giant muscle wrapped around a core of pure evil denser than the mass that led to the Big Bang. I felt it moving. My eyes were closed because I was trying to leave my body. Its tongue flicked out and touched my hand, and I hoped that I would dissolve and turn into a vapor that would float out the window and into the atmosphere and eventually return as rain. I died a thousand times over the next five minutes, as he took pictures of me with his phone. "That is so sexy," he said. "A beautiful woman and a snake—can you think of anything more primal?"

He finally removed it. "I think Larry likes you," he said. To be liked by a snake was not my greatest ambition.

Now I wish I'd thrown the snake at him. Now I wish I'd wrapped myself around the snake preemptively and choked it to death, but I stood there trying to be nice. I was still young. I still thought being cooperative was a virtue. Now I wish I'd left the house immediately and never come back, but I didn't know how to leave politely. I even went on a second date with him. He called me for months afterward, and I kept answering, because I didn't know how to make him go away.

As I got older, I stopped seeing people for how they presented themselves publicly. Some people appear nice and normal in public and then you glimpse their unsettling inner life. Friendly, safe men looked suddenly like men who would breed spiders, or sleep in a coffin, or wear a vial of blood around their neck for good luck. Strangers began to look like loaded guns, cocked and ready to fire.

◆ ◆ ◆

My job is to not be difficult. My whole life, I've done things not because I want to do them but because a good woman learns to shut her mouth and go along with it. When I was in college, I worked at an ice-cream shop with a manager named Doug who insisted I give him a hug at the end of every shift. "Time for Doug's Hugs," he would announce, and we all had to line up and hug him good night, like we were toys he played with and then put away before going to bed. He didn't know any better, my coworkers said. It wasn't worth starting a whole big thing, they said.

◆ ◆ ◆

In a country that I couldn't locate on the map, a school was raided and all the children were kidnapped by a terrorist group.

The boys were featured in propaganda videos, smiling with gaps in their teeth as a powerful bearded man handed them assault rifles and had them point at a target, on which they'd affixed a picture of our president. The terrorists are all boys, armed with God and guns and hate and desperation. If they'd been born in another place, they might spend their evenings chatting with girls online and watching music videos and generating endless variations on memes. They would spend their mornings cramming for geometry tests and repeating lines from movies to their friends and sneaking out of class to have a cigarette. They would sometimes have an active-shooter drill, where they would practice hiding from a madman with a gun. They would have pizza for lunch and they would go to track practice after school. They would eat dinner with their parents and watch popular sitcoms. But they were born in the wrong place at the wrong time, and that's all that matters. Now they sell heroin and they sell girls so they can buy more guns and explosives and most of those boys will die before they turn twenty. Some will do it intentionally, because they've been told it is God's will.

The girls would become sex slaves. They would be forced to cook and clean and fuck these men who had declared war on the entire world. In our country, there was talk of rescuing them, but it seemed beyond impossible. Every few weeks, they show you a picture of a person you never knew existed. They say, "He was a very bad man." They say, "We killed him." They say this makes you safer. And you have to believe them because either you're safer or you're not.

• • •

In Rome, someone drove a truck into a crowd that was watching a soccer game in a public square. One of the major terrorist groups had claimed responsibility, but then another group did too, and nobody could agree who should get credit for the deaths. Nobody could agree who the enemy was. The truck had injured ten people and killed six. On the news, they called it a bloodbath. The average body holds eight pints of blood and the average bathtub holds about 40 gallons of liquid. For something to be rightly called a bloodbath, then 320 pints of blood would need to be spilled, or forty whole humans' worth. The truck attack barely qualified. It was more like a blood sink. It's important to be precise, to know exactly how much blood there is and how much is being spilled. You don't want to sensationalize it.

A group of senators began pushing for a preemptive war. Wars start because powerful men get bored and they get old. They're afraid of dying so they try to kill as many people as possible while they still can. Their slogan was "Something Should Happen." They used it on social media. They hashtagged it. They repeated it on the news. The pundits agreed: a bad thing had happened and now, in response, another thing should happen. It was hard to dispute. On the question, *Should things continue to happen or should they not continue to happen?*, these senators had taken a firm stand. They refused to offer specifics on what that something should be, on the grounds that giving away their plans would only empower our enemies. But it seemed to me like what we really needed was fewer things. Things had been happening for so long and so many of them had gone badly. What if nothing happened, for a very long time? What if we agreed to stop things, in general?

• • •

When a Muslim man did the killing, the TV showed videos of groups of angry Muslim men, shouting at cameras and waving guns in the air. The pundits debated whether it was possible to trust someone who believed in the god they believed in. When a black man did the killing, they asked why other black men weren't doing more to stop them. They interviewed sociologists about what had caused such corruption in the souls of young black men. When a white man did the killing, they called him a lone wolf. The white male lone wolf is an apex predator. Lone wolves stalk our suburbs and our schools and they aren't in sheep's clothing, they're out in the open.

• • •

Is there a total amount of violence that can be spread throughout the planet at a given time? Is there even a point in remembering the names of the victims? We didn't hear about most of the carnage overseas. We only got international news when something nightmarish happened. If it was terrorism, then they told us about it, and they told us it could come here next. They asked what our leaders were doing to combat terror. They used terror as a noun, a verb, an adjective. They wore terror like a suit of armor. There are only so many massacres you can handle before you lose hope. The world is in a prolonged state of massacre and the only thing we can do is try not to see it all at once.

◆ ◆ ◆

The president would arrive in a week. Seldom Falls had begun security preparations, closing streets, towing cars, installing even more cameras. We received letters from local officials about how to stay safe during this visit. They said to avoid the area entirely, to stay with relatives outside of town if possible. Calvin must have been reading the same news as me, because he called the next night and said, "You can stay with me if you need to get out of town."

I told him I was just going to lay low. I didn't tell him I was at Robbie's place, or that Robbie existed. I didn't want either of them to know about the other. It seemed too complicated.

"Listen," he said. "I've been thinking. What if you move out here?"

"This is not a good time to talk about things like that."

"You could stay with us until you find your own place. We could actually see each other."

I hung up. I searched my phone for a button to undo the conversation I'd just had, but I could not find it. Technology does so many things, but almost none of them are useful.

◆ ◆ ◆

The media descended on us two days before the president arrived. I stayed at Robbie's apartment, hoping they wouldn't be able to find me. A producer for one of the major networks had been leaving me voicemails every day for the past month. She wanted to give me an opportunity to tell my side of the story. I closed the blinds and sat inside our cushion bomb shelter and tried to be inconspicuous. Robbie wouldn't turn the TV off. He was fascinated by watching video of places he saw every day.

"Babe," he said. "Check it out: they're over by Eddie's house." He turned the volume up so I could hear his friend being interviewed. The reporter wanted to know if he thought the town was healing. Eddie said everyone was more cautious now, but he thought we had all become stronger than ever. He repeated the slogan Mayor Randy had been promoting: "We Will Not Be Defeated." Eddie added that he'd been praying more lately. He said God has a plan for us all. "Oh wow, I have to text him," Robbie said when the segment ended.

I took the remote and changed the channel.

"Come on, don't be like that," Robbie said. "You have to see the fun in this."

• • •

People think I don't have a sense of humor, but I have one. Here's a joke:

A gun walks into a bar. The bartender pours it a beer and says, "You new in town?" then the gun shoots him in the face because it is a gun.

• • •

Someone knocked on Robbie's door. I thought it might be Angie or Reverend Chet; I had been avoiding their phone calls since the gun show. I'd failed to buy their guns and I knew they would probably excommunicate me. Robbie checked the peephole.

"It's some guy in a suit," he said, too loudly. Whoever was on the other side of the door must have heard him. We watched the shadow beneath the door. I listened closely enough that I could hear the visitor's phone dinging every time he received another text message.

What kind of suited men just show up knocking on strange doors at night? Jehovah's Witnesses. Government agents. Satan. The landlord.

The man knocked again.

"Ms. Crawford," he called. "I just want to talk to you."

Nobody just wants to talk.

"I'm from CNN," he said. "I want to tell your story."

We waited until midnight, and every time Robbie checked, the reporter was still there. He suggested calling the police, but I didn't want them near me. The police had already cut me open once and left without stitching me back together. The thought of their hands on me again made me nauseous.

The man in the hall slipped a note under the door saying, "I come in peace."

He knew he could wait us out. He knew if he pressured me long enough, I would crack and give him an interview just to get him away from me. He was a man with ambition and an expense account; this made him one of the planet's most dangerous predators.

When he came inside, he shook my hand and introduced himself as Artis McLellan. He was so young he looked like he'd have to wake up in a few hours to take his SATs and then go to soccer practice. I don't know when I got old enough to notice how young people looked.

He'd found me because Robbie had posted a picture of me online, sleeping in the fort. He said I'd looked cute and he wanted to share. "People should see a better side of you," he said. I had pulled all of my social media pages down after my arrest, but Artis told me that most of them don't actually go away, they just get harder to find. As he spoke, I considered the exact ways in which I would kill Robbie, the places where I would hide his limbs after I dismembered him, the look of terror in his eyes as I did it.

Artis spoke to me for an hour. He wanted to know how the town had changed and what we hoped for in the future. He avoided the word "shooting." He did not say "murder." Robbie sometimes interjected with his own answers. "I think she's just scared, like all of us," Robbie said.

Scared. It sounds like the emotion of a child. You get scared of a spider.

Artis asked, "What lessons do you think the town has learned from this ordeal?"

Lessons.

As if we'd just graduated and become American grown-ups because we'd finally bathed in the blood of our neighbors. "I don't understand the question," I said.

"What I mean is, would you say this has ultimately made the town stronger?"

Robbie nodded, said, "I really think it has. It's like, one

day things are terrible and the next they're a little better, but eventually you learn how to cope, you know? It's really brought people together."

"Do bullets make you stronger?" I said. "Do you think it's better to get shot or not get shot?"

Artis looked to Robbie in that conspiratorial way men have to say, *What's with the crazy bitch?* Robbie shrugged.

"Listen," Artis said. "People don't want stories about how sad people are. They want *uplift*. They want to feel better."

◆ ◆ ◆

The president landed at the military air base at seven a.m., then his convoy drove him to Main Street. There, he would take a tour of three local businesses—a bakery, a diner, and an antique shop. People loved pastries and lunch and old things, in that order. At ten o'clock, he would take the stage at the center of the high school football field.

Even though I arrived early, it was crowded enough that I needed binoculars to see him onstage. I didn't need to listen to his words because I had already heard him say the same things before. Behind him, the ghosts sat in the windows and watched, but their faces were emotionless. They looked exactly like students enduring a boring lecture about foreshadowing. They did not care what he said.

Because people were afraid he was going to take their guns away, many showed up to his events fully armed. They said it was not a threat. They were just exercising their God-given right to imply murder. They were just reminding everyone of what they could have done if they'd wanted to. Then there was the pocket of counter-protesters, some of whom had smeared fake blood on their faces and dressed as the victims of a shooting. They held signs saying WHO'S NEXT?

Afterward, the president toured the grounds while media followed and filmed him looking thoughtfully at the places where people had died. He stood in front of the school, head bowed as a priest led us in prayer, and then he was hustled to his car.

One news network criticized him for not taking a strong enough stance against guns, and another said he was the most divisive president in history. They said he was a dictator, and they said Hitler started small too. They suggested he was actually endangering gun owners with his inflammatory rhetoric. On a third network, they talked to a medium who had done freelance investigative work for the police and asked her where she thought the next shooting would take place.

◆ ◆ ◆

Is there a war on guns? The woman on the TV wanted to know. "I'm not saying there is," she said. "I'm just asking the question." Should guns feel threatened? The only way to kill a gun is to cut off the hand attached to it, but there are so many hands.

◆ ◆ ◆

Another truck attack occurred in another European city, and I began to regret all the years I'd spent not fearing automobiles. You grow up surrounded by them and you use them every day and so you forget how easily and how often they kill people. First we had paths for our horses then we had small roads for our cars then we had interstate highways, then we started dying at unprecedented rates because it became very important to get to our destinations very quickly. Massive roads are a testament to human ambition, but ambition is what kills you fastest. I wrote a letter to the editor at the *Seldom Falls Herald* saying we should ban cars. Not just cars, but trucks and motorcycles and anything with an engine. We should close all the roads, I said, make them impassable and plant grass over them and become a society of pedestrians again. We should embrace the natural limits imposed on us by biology; in your life, you only get to travel as far as your own body will take you and then that's it. The worst thing that ever happened was when men started sailing across the globe to find new places to visit and own and destroy. No other animal is so self-destructive in its migration.

• • •

Ban everything besides guns. Ban public space. Ban buildings. Ban trigger fingers. Ban anger. Ban flesh and organs and blood loss. Ban women and children who are easy targets and ban men who like to shoot at targets. Ban physics, and ban velocity. Ban human interaction.

HOW TO BE SAFE, PART II

MAKE YOURSELF LOOK bigger than a cougar. Raise your arms above your head like a taxidermied grizzly. Purchase clothing that exaggerates your size: thick-soled boots, trench coats, top hats, baggy T-shirts with horizontal stripes. It is essential to look big because if you don't look big then you look small, and if you look small then you look exploitable. Some venomous snakes and spiders are small and dangerous, but they are the exception and you are no snake. You are no spider. You are just a person without claws or a venom sac or fangs or built-in camouflage. Your bones feel hard at first, but even mountains crumble under enough pressure. All it takes is a moderately bad fall to break your bones, to release fluid that will pool up around your heart and in your lungs. Your skin rips. Your tissue melts. Your organs are soft, meaty targets. You don't have a sixth sense that can protect you. Your five senses barely work, relative to the rest of nature.

WEAR REFLECTIVE CLOTHING. You want cars to be able to see you when you're walking around your neighborhood, in an effort to strengthen your legs and your lungs, to improve your outlook on life, which seems like the sort of thing that should happen if you walk around your neighborhood, because the people who do that all appear happy or at least happy enough. Never walk at night—at night, there is an increased risk of drunk drivers on the road, plus the darkness makes it harder to avoid tripping hazards, not to mention the muggers and rapists and, on certain nights, the werewolves. REFLECTIVE CLOTHING DOES NOT REPEL WERE-WOLVES. But it does help drivers to see the moonlight bounce off your vest and sneakers and the adhesive strips you've attached to your walking pants.

SELF-MEDICATE WHENEVER POSSIBLE. Whatever drug is helping you to cope is one that will kill you but at least you're maintaining some control over how and when you go.

DECEMBER

AFTER THE JOURNALISTS were done investigating the boy's house, the scholars had their chance to study it, and then it became a tourist attraction. With Sylvia dead and the mortgage unpaid, the property was assumed by the bank, and the bank wanted to make its money back by charging admission. They promised an insider's view of the environment that creates a monster. Massacre tourism was one of the biggest growth markets in the economy. Small towns across the country allow people to be murdered and then later the local economy benefits from travelers wandering through town for a couple days before heading off to the next site of a mass murder. When industry dies, you need to replace the revenue somehow. Some people tried to predict the next mass shooting based on risk factors and traveled to the sites in anticipation, like tornado hunters chasing funnel clouds.

This is what the boy's room looked like: there was a laptop open to a popular message board where teens shared racist jokes, stolen pornography, and conspiracy theories. There was a mound of discarded clothing in the corner. A pile of books on the bedside table—exactly the books a smart but pretentious teenage boy would own: Nietzsche, Kerouac, Bukowski, Jim Morrison's poetry. There was a video-game system and a stack of games in which the protagonist's job is to murder as many people as possible as creatively as possible. A half-empty pack of cigarettes. It was a profoundly uninteresting room. It was a monument to banality.

On the day I went, I was the only visitor. My guide was a man named Herman, who told me he'd wanted to work as a docent in the national museums in DC but had failed the background check. He was doing his time here until another opportunity came along. Why had he failed the background check? "You know how it is," he said.

Herman said, "You want to see something really interesting?" When you're alone with a man and he asks if you want to see something interesting, it's reasonable to worry that he's talking about his penis. Men think their penises are much more interesting than they actually are. As soon as Adam discovered his erection, the world was doomed. He tried to put it inside Eve, and even though she wasn't sure, she let him because it seemed easier that way. And then he was so proud of himself, like he'd invented something. All he wanted was admiration for his erection and when he didn't get it, he lashed out.

I told Herman I was fine not seeing something interesting.

"Come on," he said. He put his arm on my shoulder, leading me toward the bed. I decided then that I would murder him if he pushed me onto the bed or his hand moved anywhere besides exactly where it was. I would blame it on the psychic energy of the room.

He leaned down and lifted up the mattress. There were five DVDs beneath it. "He kept porn in here." Herman laughed. "Kid had decent taste." The only thing I wanted in the world was to not have a conversation about contraband porn with Herman. "Kids have it easier now," he said. "I had to go out in the woods where my friends had hid a *Playboy* under a rock. We had to steal it from my friend's grampa, who kept it in a box with all this old World War Two stuff. Nowadays, they can get whatever they want online." He quietly contemplated the lost erections of his youth.

To get whatever you want whenever you want is a luxury of the future. You want things and you get them and then you feel sick of them and then you want to die.

Herman wanted to show me one more thing, in the closet. The boy had owned many stuffed animals, all of which had been crammed into a box. I imagined the boy waking up on the morning he was going to die and opening his closet to dig out his clothes for the day. He knew what he was going to wear, had planned it for months. He stepped into his camouflage pants and checked to make sure the cargo pockets were still packed with ammo. He'd stashed a backpack full of homemade explosives in the back of the closet. After he strapped it on, he leaned forward and saw the container filled with his animals. I imagined him picking up the stuffed elephant—the elephant's name was Spout; it was written on the tag—and pressing his lips together to make a sound like an elephant's trumpeting. Spout had been his favorite toy for years, even after he was old enough to have outgrown stuffed animals, and I could see the areas where his exterior was faded and worn by years of play. He'd put these animals away reluctantly. Until recently, they had been scattered across his bed, had lain with him when he was sick with the flu, had comforted him as he tried to fall asleep despite the tsunami of rage in his head. But he'd gotten older, and there was always the possibility of a girl coming to his room, and also he felt self-conscious sitting at his computer with his back to them while he researched the most efficient means of killing large groups of people. He still checked on them most mornings. Still grabbed their little arms and made them wave to him, still rearranged them in their box to make them more comfortable. As he practiced deep-breathing exercises in his room, mentally preparing himself to become a martyr, he realized he wouldn't miss his mother or his computer or his pornography or his few friends, but he would miss Spout and Stella and Gus and the dozens of others he had loved more than he'd ever loved any person. He pushed them deeper into the box and tried to fold the flap shut, as if to hide them from hearing the news, but also he knew they would notice when he never returned. And they would not be donated to needy children or used in any good way because they would be viewed, like everything in this room, as tainted, as relics of an evil person.

"No, look behind the box," Herman said. "Behind it."

On the floor behind the boxes was a cache of liquor bottles.

"He must have had five hundred dollars' worth of booze here."

I didn't understand why it hadn't been confiscated. Herman said he took a couple drinks each day to keep himself loose. He took a swig straight from a plastic bottle of vodka before offering it to me. Just that morning I'd promised myself I would go a day without drinking. I wanted to be clear-headed. I wanted to wake up one morning that week and feel good about myself. But it was there and he was relentless and so I sipped it, my lips on the same bottle from which the boy himself had drunk. I felt the boy then in my blood. I felt him working through my veins. I took another sip. The boy was taking up residence inside my body, so that I could feel how alone and terrified and violated he'd felt. For a moment I was an archangel on a path of divine vengeance and all I wanted was to see something burn. I held a flaming sword in my hands and pictured it cutting through the hearts of my enemies. I thought I should force myself to vomit and run out of this house so that he wouldn't be inside me any longer. My head was light and my mouth was tingling, and I wanted more of that feeling. Herman and I continued drinking, standing the whole time in front of the bed. The boy inside both of us, his rage and fear inside both of us.

◆ ◆ ◆

The boys are victims too. They're taught to act a certain way and that the one means to being a man is to prove themselves through bloodshed. They're exposed to the Old Testament first and they never forget that even God will kill his people over petty slights. They are handed a thousand problems and only one solution and then they are told to figure it out on their own.

. . .

The next morning, or maybe it was several mornings later, I woke up in my bed and I found myself clutching the guestbook from the boy's home. H. Renfroe and family from Charleston had visited and they wrote, *Chilling!* L. Riggs from Ontario said, *Great site!* P. Logan from Indianapolis said, *Makes You Think*.

. . .

Calvin got in the habit of just texting me three question marks when he was worried about me. Every few days: *???* would show up on my phone. This time, I had to decide how to tell him I wasn't going to go to his house for Christmas. I'd never had Christmas dinner with his family before. I didn't know their traditions. I was afraid that spending even one day with Harlan and Colleen would make me love them in the same way I loved my brother. My mother's distance had taught me that it's better to love people from afar. Calvin would be disappointed. He was always disappointed. My job was to dial ten numbers, listen to the ringing, and when my brother answered, to say, "Merry Christmas, Calvin." My job on Christmas was to call him and to talk to him for exactly one half of one hour. To ask about his children and his wife. To ask how work was going. To see if he was looking forward to the upcoming year. To reassure him I was doing well and then tell him a lie about how I was going to be spending the day with friends. Instead of calling, I manufactured chores to keep myself distracted. I took long drives to outlet malls to buy items I didn't need. I fucked Robbie ferociously until he asked me to stop. I cultivated an abiding interest in maintaining the cleanliness of my windows. I removed half the wallpaper in my bathroom.

• • •

December is a time for observing traditions, even if you don't believe in them. It doesn't make sense to bring a dead tree into your house and cover it in very hot lights, but we do it anyway. It's important to be close to your family even when you're not close to them. Even that year, I had put the old decorations out, without even thinking. The snowmen and the Santas and the candy canes all over my walls, on my shelves. I was being festive. I was filling myself with the Christmas spirit. I was trying.

• • •

Every resident of Seldom Falls was required to sign up for an emergency alert registry. We gave them our phone numbers and email addresses, and they said they wouldn't use that information to track us, but I knew they would be tracking us. They sent a text message and an email anytime there was an emergency, and in the case of what they called *an extreme danger event* they called us too. The first weekend, they tested the system three times, and each time the phone buzzed I panicked and felt my stomach folding in on itself. I received messages every few days, about a robbery a few miles away or a stolen car or a break-in. I had never thought of these issues as town-wide emergencies before, but now I felt beset by crime. I began seeing my neighbors not as people but as either victims or perpetrators. At first I thought I wanted to know about every danger around me, but I found myself paralyzed by it. There was an option to unsubscribe from the alerts, but what if the next one was about an extreme danger event? What if Godzilla came to town and I was the only one who didn't know?

◆ ◆ ◆

A few years into my teaching career, during a school assembly near the end of the semester, I was called onstage by the entertainer, who was a magician. There was a spotlight on me and people chanting my name. There was too much pressure for me not to go along with it. I took the long walk to the stage, past guffawing children, who, I realized at that moment, hated me, and wanted to see me humiliated.

I tried to be a good sport. I did that raise-the-roof motion people used to do; even as my hands were moving, I realized this made me look like I was ancient. When you're onstage, you become suddenly very conscious of the placement of your hands. As I held them primly against my side, I wished I'd never had hands, that I'd been born armless and legless and torso-less.

The magician made me sit in a chair in the middle of the stage. He put his hand on my face—on my *face*—and I felt all the cells on that side of my body straining to break free. He asked if I'd ever been hypnotized before. He went through the preamble about how I would get sleepy and so on, and as I was thinking about how much I wanted to escape, I did find myself getting sleepy. I left my body and ceded control of it to him. I was still mentally there, but in a cage inside my brain. I could see everything happening, but I couldn't do anything about it. He made me stand and jump and do push-ups and hide under a table as if an atom bomb was about to fall. He made me squeal like a pig and roll around in pretend mud and kiss the principal on the mouth. He said, "When I snap my fingers, you will tell us one very private secret." I couldn't stop myself from announcing that through college I had worked as a phone sex operator to make extra cash. The response was deafening. I would rather have died.

I'm not embarrassed to have worked phone sex lines. The men who called me were lonely. They wanted someone to pretend to like them. I needed money, and I was good at making myself into the woman they wanted. I have done much more degrading things for money, like waiting tables. But when strangers hear about what I did they provide the shame for me. They do an impression of the breathy phone sex voice. They ask questions about the weirdest conversations I've ever heard. They think about my mouth forming filthy words to help a stranger get off, and their perception of me changes. As a teacher in a high school, there is no worse information to give away to herds of boys who are obsessed with their penises. They suddenly see you as attainable and forget that you're a person. The girls see you as pitiful, as a cautionary tale.

Since the hypnotism, I have been two people: one who does things she cannot control, and one who hates the other person. My online therapist told me I was displacing blame. Robbie said this was the kind of drama he couldn't handle. He said it would be easier if I just accepted responsibility for my actions.

• • •

Robbie suggested a vacation. It had been a very bad year, and he thought it would be good for both of us to end it with something nice. To treat ourselves. But the thought of getting on a plane made me ill. "During these troubled times," I said, trying to sound as rational as possible, "Does it really strike you as sensible for us to get on a plane? To be surrounded by strangers? *In the air?*" Imagine it. Robbie reminded me that we had once gone to a Caribbean resort together, the first time we'd been dating. He reminded me how the most difficult decision every day had been which drink to order with breakfast. How we'd spent hours by the pool and then had lazy, drunken sex all night. I remembered a version of myself having done such a thing, but couldn't believe it had been me. To be in a plane? It felt like a death sentence.

• • •

My online therapist said I needed to be willing to compromise, so I agreed to drive with Robbie to Ohio for a long weekend. We were going to stay at a bed and breakfast and get away from it all. Adults go on weekend getaways all the time. It's a normal thing normal people do.

About thirty miles outside of Seldom Falls, we saw the sun again, cutting through a thick blanket of clouds. To feel it on my skin again, to feel enveloped by it, made me feel human. I lowered the window and stretched both my arms outside. I wanted to climb up onto the roof and strip naked and cover myself in sunlight.

Robbie drove erratically because he couldn't stop fiddling with the radio. Nobody noticed, because that's how everyone else was driving. From the passenger seat on the highway, you can see that nobody is looking at the road. They are all looking at their phones. "Cars are too easy to drive," I said. "It should be harder to use something that can kill you."

"Huh?"

"Nothing."

Robbie sighed. "Christ. Come on, just tell me," he said. The car slowed as he stared at me. "Don't get mad just because I don't hear every single thing you say."

"It wasn't important."

"You mutter. You know? You mutter and you grind your teeth."

"I don't want to talk about my teeth." I turned the radio up.

Robbie asked me to open the glove compartment. Inside, there was a pile of napkins, a Bible, and a brown lunch bag. "Check the bag," he said. He looked very proud of himself.

The bag contained two smaller baggies, one containing pot, and the other a number of unmarked pills. "Don't I feel like a princess," I said. "A lunch bag full of loose drugs."

"Why do you make it so hard to do something nice for you?"

"I guess I'm just difficult," I said, shoving the bag back into the glove compartment.

"I thought it would be fun? Get a little crazy?"

"So you filled my car with drugs and drove it across state lines."

He honked the horn and held it in.

"You can't honk at someone who's inside the car," I said.

He honked again. "Could you just—" He paused to check the directions on his phone. "Could you just cooperate on something? It's exhausting trying to manage you."

Women are supposed to be fluffy clouds that glide through men's lives when it's convenient for them. So, fine: I reached into the bag and swallowed two of the pills and waited to see what would happen.

• • •

The innkeeper was an older man who kept referring to his wife as "my bride," and who had the unpleasant habit of addressing us as "kids."

"Kids, follow me," he said. My face tingled like a limb regaining feeling and my tongue felt like a dead thing lying inside my mouth. Robbie didn't know exactly what pills I'd taken. A friend had given them to him with the promise that we would have a lot of fun. Robbie and the innkeeper spoke to each other. I registered their voices, but as soon as the words entered my ears they splintered and sent disconnected letters spiraling through my brain. I could see all the letters piling up in the landfill of my mind, and I imagined my other self standing there, her hand thrust deep into my skull, sorting through like an archaeologist and trying to make sense of everything inside.

Robbie led me away from the conversation and then we were in the room. My right arm was glued to my side. My hair felt hot.

I was trying to be fun. I was trying to be flirty. I wasn't opposed to being these things. During the four days in the B&B, we spent a lot of time in the room, where there was a large soaking tub and a fireplace. We took pills and smoked pot and drank a bottle of wine a day. We sat naked in the tub for hours.

When Robbie was asleep, I read the old guest books. One woman wrote that she'd taken her husband here for their fiftieth anniversary. "I believe this stay saved our marriage," she said. "Ever since the kids, we've never had time to ourselves, and your beautiful home brought back the man I loved." Fifty years of marriage seemed beyond impossible, almost selfish. To even live fifty years was a miracle. What would I have done if I'd lived in a home with two happily married parents who stayed together for fifty years and told cute stories about their courtship? Would other people like that now invite me to their house on weekends for lunch and fill me in on their neighborhood gossip? Would I volunteer at town meetings to organize festivals and craft fairs? The guestbook was filled with liars. I crossed out their notes and changed them to make them more truthful. I changed one couple's note to say, "I just came here to have sex in a new bed." Another I changed to: "At night, I pretend I'm a whale, separated from my pod and lost on land, trying to blend in with the humans and surviving just barely, and while I'm here in this room I can stop pretending and just lie in the bathtub and believe I'm at home with my family."

◆ ◆ ◆

Breakfast was served in a community seating arrangement. "Like the Europeans," the innkeeper said. He placed his hand on my shoulder while he spoke. I was desperately thirsty and drank three glasses of water before he gave me my own pitcher. The three other couples at the table were all married. Dull conversation assaulted me from all angles. I said very little.

Where do people get stories? Do they go out in the world looking for interesting anecdotes? When they get home, do they write these things down and rehearse them?

"You two are still so young," one man said. His hair was thick and shiny and had a natural curl that many women would kill for. The spots on his hands showed his age but he was still one of the handsomest men I'd ever met. He had a voice like a news anchor. He said he did government work. "Wait till you get to our age," he said, and all the other couples laughed for some reason. There is nothing old people enjoy more than telling younger people exactly how old they are. I ate eggs and bacon and drank water and eventually left mid-conversation.

The last thing we did in Ohio was visit a psychic named Madame Cordova. Everything in the room was white—carpet, walls, couch, pillows, a puffy little dog she said was from Siberia and descended from Lenin's dogs. She told us to close our eyes and then held our hands. She made the kinds of spirit-summoning noises psychics make. Energy hummed through my arms. It was hard to keep my eyes closed, but sometimes it feels good to follow orders. She abruptly pulled away from us. "I've seen all I need to see," she said, and walked out of the room. We waited ten minutes, assuming she would come back with some information, or a potion, or something, but she didn't.

◆ ◆ ◆

At a rest stop, I stood at the bathroom sink studying the posters on the walls warning travelers to be on the lookout for human trafficking. watch for the signs, they said, but they didn't say what the signs were. I tried to determine whether I looked like I had been trafficked. Was I showing the signs? Were the other women here of their own volition? Before looking at the poster, I hadn't considered the possibility that I was surrounded by sex slaves. On the highway, you can run into more dangers than you've ever imagined. Not just distracted drivers but stalkers, sex traffickers, teens throwing rocks through windshields from the overpass. If you pass enough cars, you will have passed at least one murderer; that's just statistics.

* * *

The day our vacation ended, I returned to the mysterious confession booth outside Murphy's Law. I waited my turn in line at the booth and I sat down and then I unloaded my sins. I told the story of the time I was supposed to feed my vacationing neighbor's cat and clean the litter box, but instead I just let it out in the backyard, and later I told the neighbors someone must have broken in and stolen it. I said I hadn't paid any bills on time in years. I recited all the daily chores I'd left undone; everyone else seemed so organized and well prepared and I felt like I was always scrambling to catch up. I said I was lazy and unfocused and I understood why I was unlovable, but I still wished it weren't so. Then I said sometimes at night I think maybe I'm actually the one who did the shooting. I felt I was responsible somehow.

My confessor asked if I'd called my brother yet.

I didn't call him until New Year's Eve. I told him I was sorry I hadn't made it to his place for Christmas.

"What are you avoiding?" he said. "Did I do something?"

"It's just busy around here. I have a busy life."

"Here's the deal. If you can't come here, I'm coming to you. Dr. Falk says I need to strengthen my bonds."

The last time my brother and I had been together in Seldom Falls, I was testifying on his behalf as a character witness for the parole board. I didn't know how to stop him from coming back this time.

JANUARY

SINCE SEPTEMBER, the high school students had been redistributed to other schools in the area, but nobody was happy with that solution. They'd been randomly assigned to their temporary schools, so friendships were fractured and relationships ended; sometimes the only thing keeping two people together is scheduling. The staff at the new schools complained that our students were disciplinary problems. They said these students weren't temperamentally suited to their new environments, and also they were a burden on their curriculum. Our teachers and staff were out of work, and the township had only agreed to pay them for emergency leave for one month. School psychologists said the worst possible way to handle the situation was to displace the students and subject them to even more upheaval. But there was the problem of the bodies and blood and the bullets. It takes a long time to scrub a massacre site, and you can only do that after all the evidence is collected. The cleanup had ended a week before Christmas. All the holes had been patched and the walls repainted and the floors, buckled by water damage, were replaced. Everyone was desperate to get back to normal. But normal doesn't exist. You develop nostalgia first for your youth then for a fictional time that looks like your youth but was never real.

• • •

Before the shooting, I hadn't even known who my government representatives were. I was not a voter. I considered myself intelligent, but also busy. I was just informed enough to feel like there was no point in participating, to invite the betrayal of politicians, who were not even human. They were excellent at replicating human emotion but not at understanding how real people felt or behaved. In the months after the shooting, the state senator from my district had built himself into a national figure. Every murder is an opportunity for someone else to succeed. He said his divine mission was to protect our state's children. He made regular TV appearances promising to solve the murder problem once and for all. Most other state officials remained silent. They'd learned a long time ago that the best way to stay in power is to remind people you even have power only when it's absolutely necessary. True leadership is never having an opinion on anything, because opinions might upset people.

The state senator pushed to eliminate the restrictions on concealed carrying on school grounds. He said it would be dangerously negligent for the teachers to return to work unarmed. On the legislature floor, he stood silently beside posters of the victims, their smiling faces. On the bottom of the images was white text: *#NeverAgain*

A week before the school reopened, they enacted a new policy: every teacher and administrator would be required to keep a gun at their desk, like blackjack dealers in the Old West, and in each grade, ten students would be designated as Class Guardians, armed and trained in tactical shooting. "Criminals will always have guns," the state senator said. "It's up to us to outnumber them with our own guns." Given the option, he probably would have installed cannons at the entrance. He probably would have torn down the building and replaced it with a giant gun. He would have lived inside the barrel of a gun and fired himself into the chest of suspects.

• • •

Our state senator had partnered with the previous president and three of the world's five largest corporations to form an antiviolence task force. "As of this day," our state senator said, "we are declaring an all-out war on violence."

The front lines of the war on violence were in commercials, and in sponsored content on websites. There was a hotline to call. There were bumper stickers. There were many speeches. I watched videos of well-dressed, handsome men on daises talking about their hatred of violence, and I wondered how many had had dreams of driving a knife into the belly of their neighbor. How many had tried to run a car off the road because they'd been cut off. How many were sitting there quietly and scanning the crowd looking for the woman they most wanted to fuck.

◆ ◆ ◆

Angie Sparks and Reverend Chet were in my house. They wanted to know why I hadn't purchased the guns I'd promised to purchase. I told them I didn't think I was cut out for the apocalypse. I was sorry for having made a promise I knew I couldn't keep. In the infinite possible timelines in which I exist, no version of me would be capable of standing up to the Four Horsemen when they arrived.

Reverend Chet paced in circles. "This is a grave disappointment," he said. "I was under the impression that you were ready to be saved." Angie shook her head at me. She followed Chet around the room. "I thought we'd found a kindred spirit. I thought you understood that your soul is on the line. The expiration date is coming soon," he said. He raised his voice, "Doomsday is imminent! And you can't be bothered to help us?"

They'd been nice to me, at least until they'd tried to pressure me into buying guns I didn't want. But a brief period of niceness before the cruelty is the best you can ask for from some people. "I'm sorry I can't help you," I said, and I'd meant it. I wanted very badly to be able to fully immerse myself in a group like this. They had such a clear sense of purpose.

Angie glared at me. "I tried to save you," she said. "And you wasted my time."

◆ ◆ ◆

As the anniversary of the shooting approached, progress on the memorial had stalled. Construction had been delayed, restarted, and delayed again. No one could agree on what the memorial should look like, who should be honored, or where it should be placed. Death doesn't belong to the dead. It belongs to the people it leaves behind. Memorials are vanity projects anyway. They are slabs of stone painstakingly crafted into slightly different slabs. They are created at the height of despair and then later regretted, then forgotten. The first time I ran away from home, I was only gone for twelve hours, and I spent most of my time in the woods behind the high school. I uncovered a granite slab the size of a large shoebox. It was a memorial to local veterans of the Spanish-American war. Seventeen names were carved into it. I found a man with my last name, and traced my finger over the letters, trying to have a meaningful moment with it, this discovery of a perhaps long-lost relative named Earl. But Earl Crawford was an abstraction, no matter how concrete they tried to make him. The war itself was an abstraction. Memorials mean less with each day that passes. Two decades from now, the freshmen in this school will see the shooting memorial and think nothing of it. They will lean against it while they sneak cigarettes. Someone will have sex on it. The urgency will be gone; you can't force people to remember. By then, a hundred more schools will have been shot up.

Everyone wants to remember forever, but the only healthy thing to do is to forget.

· · ·

At the site of every mass shooting, they were racing to build their own memorials. They felt obligated to commemorate the worst moment in their town's history. It was supposed to be about healing. It was supposed to be about remembering. But no matter how much time and money these cities spent on the design, they all came up with the same ideas. Plaques and flower gardens and small sculptures engraved with an inspirational quote. Candles and places for sitting and reflecting. Water features. The names of the victims printed on bricks. Everything was very tasteful and safe and simple. Each memorial represented a collective commitment not to remembering, but to whitewashing the memories, to creating a more palatable version of the memory for ourselves to hold on to and repeat and eventually accept as the truth. The memorials were there to hide failures, not to be critical of them. Every memory is false, and with each subsequent remembering, it becomes even more false.

◆ ◆ ◆

On a telephone pole near my house, I saw a flyer asking for volunteers for a neighborhood watch group called the Peacekeepers. Telephone poles suspend millions of miles of wires across the country, but sometimes the easiest way to communicate is to just staple a piece of paper to the pole itself. Later, I would email Norm, the organizer, and my message would travel through who knows how many miles of underground cables. Most of the structures that support our daily lives are invisible. I'd come to rely on so many things I could never describe but whose absence I would feel deeply if they were taken away.

• • •

I was the only volunteer to show up for the first meeting of the Peacekeepers. We met in Norm's garage, where he maintained a fastidious workbench and had also installed a urinal in the far wall. "For when inside's too far away," he explained. He was sitting in a lawn chair in the garage when I arrived. He dipped into the cooler by his side and handed me a can of Busch, and pointed at the empty chair next to him. He wore a shirt that said M.A.D.D. at the top and MEN AGAINST DAUGHTERS DATING at the bottom. He was in his sixties, but still trim and with active gray eyes. His mustache was so thick it eclipsed his mouth. "I was expecting a more impressive turnout," he said.

I said I was too.

Norm told me he'd been living in Seldom Falls for forty years, though I'd never seen him before. "I'm tired of looking over my shoulder everywhere I go," he said, and I agreed. He asked if I wouldn't mind taking minutes for the meeting. That way, when people joined later, they would be able to get up to speed more quickly. I had not intended to be the secretary, but I didn't seem to have a choice.

Later, when I checked my notes, they said:

> <u>Meeting 1</u>
> *Goals:* Make neighborhood safe again.
> *Methods:* ?
> *Recruitment:* ?
> *Next meeting:* order pizza

163

• • •

Calvin was due to arrive by the end of the next week. I told him again not to come, but he didn't answer. He had taken a leave of absence from work for what he called a family emergency. I needed to clean my house before he came, but I needed to do more than that. I needed to completely reorganize it, tear it down to the bones and build a new home. I wanted him to see that I was fine. I wanted my fineness to be so overwhelming it suffocated us both.

• • •

"You've been wearing the same shirt for four days straight," Robbie said, as if I were somehow unaware of this fact. "It's pathetic."

"You don't need to point these things out," I said. "Not everybody is looking to be improved."

Robbie spit a mouthful of sunflower seeds into his cup. "You're just, like, a meteor of misery, you know? Like you just crash landed here and there's a giant sad crater in my apartment."

It didn't seem like the right time to question his metaphor, so I got up and left his apartment. Do meteors just walk away? No, they do not. They burn up in the atmosphere, or they get chipped into pocket-sized pieces by collectors and sold on the Internet.

The next day, I told Robbie I was feeling lonely in this grim, sunless town. Loneliness has a volume like any liquid. It fills you up and makes you heavier and you try to dispel it through tears, but tears replenish themselves. Loneliness has a sound, like a bird calling for its lost mate. It reverberates and bounces off the walls and every time it bounces back past you it makes your world feel smaller and smaller until at night you are pressed down to the size of an atom and unable to escape.

I told him I would rather live on the moon. Or, failing that, a different city where I knew nobody and would be free to try out a new persona. A more pleasant one. Or maybe a less pleasant one, as long as it was different.

"I, um, don't know if I can make that kind of move right now," Robbie said, and I realized he thought I was inviting him along with me. I held his hand and told him this is a me thing, not a me-and-you thing. I had to figure out where I was going.

I did not tell him about Calvin's impending visit.

◆ ◆ ◆

On the moon, your body is one-sixth of its weight on Earth, but your regrets weigh the same. The weight of your past doesn't change. It's tempting to think about moving away from Earth and leaving everything behind, but it's not practical. How would you even breathe on the moon? What would you eat?

◆ ◆ ◆

An unmanned spaceship had landed on Mars and released two data-gathering robots. The robots would work in opposite directions, so the only moment they weren't alone on that planet was the few seconds before they began working. They were going to determine whether Mars was habitable. Nobody expected to find any aliens there, but I thought: What if the aliens have been avoiding us? We always assume they're out there plotting our deaths, but it seemed much more likely to me that they'd heard all about us and decided to stay as far away as possible. If you hear there's a shark in the water, you don't go swimming. If you know there's a planet full of beings with the ambition of destroying themselves, you just go to another planet. The aliens were waiting for us to kill ourselves off so then they could move to our mostly functional planet. I began leaving my bedroom window open at night, hoping that if a UFO landed nearby, they would abduct me, take me back to wherever they'd come from.

• • •

When Calvin showed up at my house, I was painting my toenails. I'd been painting my toenails, or pretending to, for a half hour. It seemed like the kind of casual, relaxed thing happy women do. It was a good thing to be seen doing. I wanted to look like a woman in a magazine advertisement. Later, I would eat salad and laugh at nothing. I would wear white pants and dance to a song only I could hear. A woman wearing comfortable clothing and sitting on her couch while she paints her toenails cannot be an unhappy woman. Calvin filled my entire doorway. I'd forgotten how big he was; when he was thirteen, he went through a growth spurt that nearly doubled him in size. I was happy for him then, because he would finally be able to defend himself, but if you give an angry boy too much strength, he's going to break things. He smiled and spread his arms wide, calling me toward him. Calvin liked hugs. Since he'd gotten sober, it was very important to him to make physical contact with people he loved. Dr. Falk had said he'd spent his whole life avoiding intimacy. We held on to each other for a long time and I tried not to cry, but every time I saw my brother I could not get over how healthy and happy he looked, and I wanted him to know I was proud of him.

• • •

I did not know how to entertain a guest. What do most people do for fun? They look at the Internet or they look at the TV or they masturbate or they get drunk. You can do all of these things alone. I poured myself some wine and filled a glass of water for Calvin. He told me stories about going to the park with his wife and children. He talked about the great meal they'd had on Christmas.

"You can't spend the rest of your life projecting your unhappiness onto everyone else," he said. He'd learned a lot of slogans in rehab. Slogans sometimes save lives, but most often, they lead to drunks thinking they're profound.

"Thank you for your feedback," I said. "It's good to get feedback."

"I want to see the school," he said.

I knew Calvin would be able to see the ghosts as well as I could. When his addiction was at its worst, I'd heard gossip about his fights and his accidents and his constant petty crimes. I knew my brother had died a dozen times and come back, and I'd never been able to help him. Before his first car wreck, he called me, drunk, and said, "I need to know somebody will miss me," over and over again until I said, Yes, I will miss you. I knew the crash had been intentional, but the airbags had saved him. Some broken teeth, a shattered nose. Technology saves us even when we don't want it to. Someday in the future, robots will follow us like guardian angels and nobody will ever die, even when we try to kill ourselves.

I knew we would eventually go to the school together, but I felt I owed him some resistance. I felt a duty to shield him from something.

◆ ◆ ◆

Mayor Randy stationed police in SWAT gear throughout the township. He had also acquired three surveillance drones. They promise to increase security to levels that will stop all wrongdoing, but then they also promise not to inconvenience you. Somewhere in an office, there were three young people sitting behind computer screens and piloting tiny planes throughout the metro area to maintain a record of everything that was happening on the ground. The drones were unarmed, but they could summon security forces within minutes. They flew eighteen hours a day. At first, people complained that they were intrusive, but soon they started to feel comforted by the distant buzz of a circling drone. The six droneless hours every day now felt suddenly more dangerous because nobody was there to witness. Once you go out in public, you will have been recorded by somebody. And once your face is on camera, it is saved forever. Your body is distilled and spread across too many spaces. People make fun of the Amish for not wanting their pictures taken, but maybe they were always right. The camera does steal your soul, a little bit at a time.

• • •

Someone mailed a gun to a congresswoman, with a handwritten note telling her to kill herself. She had recently delivered a speech arguing that private citizens should not have access to military-grade rifles. In response to the threat, police offered a thousand-dollar reward for information leading to the capture of the criminal. A man named Richard J turned himself in, collected the cash, and then argued that arresting him for his letter was an infringement on his free speech rights. To some people, he was a hero. One of the news networks said he was a modern Patrick Henry. The next time I went to the post office, I had to have my package X-rayed, and then fill out a form promising not to do anything illegal. Everyone agreed this was a reasonable solution to the problem of men mailing guns to women they didn't like.

• • •

Calvin told me we were actually safer than ever. He showed me an article about the decrease in gun violence and another about lengthening life spans. He showed me line graphs in descent. Murder rates were down across the country. Violent crime was at its lowest point in recorded history. "A hundred years ago, no woman would expect to be able to just walk around anywhere by herself and feel safe," he said. "This is progress."

"Statistics can say anything," I said.

"There's too much information. That's the problem. You see everything and don't know how to sort it out. Only the terrible shit is memorable. But it's not all terrible."

"But what's the point of all the numbers if I happen to be in the same room as the gun when it happens again?"

"Fuck," he said. "The point is, you won't be."

Men think confidence is a virtue, but confidence is the first thing that gets you killed.

I ignored Robbie's texts while I walked around town with my brother. Robbie still did not know Calvin existed. The only thing he knew about my family was that my parents were dead, and that they'd had a bad marriage.

As we walked down Main Street, Calvin waved to familiar faces, old high school classmates, store owners, men he'd known in a different life. Even if he'd wanted to hide, he couldn't, because he still had my father's face. Enough time spent on the wrong side of the law had trained him not to trust authority, and he especially hated the drones. "Don't you feel like just climbing a wall and King Konging some of these shitty things?" he said. We'd been walking a half hour, through Main Street and down the side streets, deep into the Mud Flats, and soon we were near our old house. I don't think I led him there on purpose. I don't know who was leading. Calvin stopped talking, stopped smiling and joking as we neared our old block. He sat on the curb and lit a cigarette. "Okay, all right, that's probably enough walking for the day," he said. He looked pale and exhausted. The sickness doesn't leave you, it just takes new forms. While he lit another cigarette, I looked down the street toward the old house. I tried to see my mother and my father on the porch, but I couldn't see anything. Even when they were alive, they didn't sit together on the porch.

• • •

When I was fifteen, we hosted everyone on my father's side of the family for the first ever Crawford family reunion. I have so many aunts and uncles and cousins that I have no idea who any of them are. Prior to that reunion, I'd never met most of them, and after it, despite all the promises to keep in touch and get together more often, we never saw them again. This was when I learned that my father had two brothers, rather than just one. I knew by then that he was the type of man who would hide the existence of people. I wondered if he'd ever told anyone about me. After the reunion, I asked him why he'd never mentioned his second brother.

"I don't feel like I have to tell everyone everything," he'd said.

"Did you two get in a fight or something?"

"Anna, it's important for you to understand something. You think you know people, but you don't really know people."

I began spying on my father, expecting to find he led a secret double life. Maybe he was still having affairs, or he had a second family. Maybe he seemed so exhausted all the time because he never slept. I skipped school and sneaked back into the basement and listened to him through the floor, but all he ever did was sit in the living room and watch TV. I woke up in the middle of the night hoping to catch him sneaking out, but he was always in his bed. If he was living a double life, it was even more boring than the one he was escaping. His days of hiding and sneaking seemed long behind him.

◆ ◆ ◆

My mother's deli failed after three years because she gradually lost interest in it. Her obsessive work was derailed by sudden weekend jaunts where the family was meant to bond. We drove to Toronto and looked at the falls. While my father stood at the rail overlooking the water, my mother said to me, "He's thinking about jumping in." She laughed. "Your father is a suicide that hasn't happened yet." We went to Buffalo and to Cincinnati and to a cabin in the West Virginia mountains. I missed a lot of school. We didn't have enough money to get two hotel rooms, so my brother and I slept on a cot beside their bed. They thought I couldn't hear them, but it was all I could hear, my father rolling closer to her and pressing against her, his lips smacking on the back of her neck until she sighed and rolled over, masturbating him under the covers. I started sleeping on the floor of the closet, but still I heard them.

My mother was in the grip of some prolonged mania. Her love was aggressive and painful. We returned one Monday and found the deli in disrepair: she had forgotten to place food orders for the week and hadn't paid her employees, and so they had trashed the place. She sold it later to a man named Jensen. My mother returned to her original depressive state and we watched her wither away in front of us.

• • •

Every night, Calvin called his wife, and he told her things were going okay. He talked to his children. He told them he loved them. He was going to go home eventually, because he actually did love them. Many fathers go home every day, and many mothers do too. Many families love one another, despite everything.

VICTIMS, PART III

WHEN STUART W was a freshman, he commandeered the school's PA system and announced he was the voice of God. "I have heard your prayers," he said, and began reeling off people's requests. He identified students petitioning God for a father to come home from Afghanistan, for a dog's heart condition to be healed, for an imaginary friend to come to life, for a volcano to rise up in the middle of town, for a pair of shoes made of gold. I thought it was an innocent prank. Then he said my name: "Miss Anna Crawford, I have heard your prayers, every night, asking me to help you love yourself. This prayer and all the others, I vow to fulfill," he said before the mic suddenly cut out.

He was suspended for two weeks. When he came back, I tried to stop him and ask him if he'd really heard me, but he avoided eye contact, and he walked slowly, stiffly. They say he was bleeding on the floor of the cafeteria for three hours before he died. I don't know if he even believed in prayer.

• • •

Gilbert T started teaching at the school one year after I did, and, because I was the least tenured person on staff, I was assigned as his peer mentor. He was older than me and had been teaching for fifteen years already. When I showed him how to input grades in our computer system, he said, "Yes, I am aware of how grading works."

In the faculty lounge, he would spread his newspaper across half the table and lean over it all morning, muttering to himself and counting out letters on his fingers. He was always working on the crossword, but I'd never seen him finish one.

When he wasn't reading the paper, he was filling out promotional postcards; once a week, he went to the big chain bookstore, rifled through all the magazines, and removed the inserts to apply for various sweepstakes and giveaways. He harvested fifty at a time. One day, I asked him how often he won. "I never send them in," he said. "What's the point? With my luck." Then he continued filling one out. I imagined a room in his house full of unsent sweepstakes entries. I wondered if the stack itself had any cash value. He wasn't killed in the shooting, but he couldn't walk, and he'd lost so much blood that his cognitive function was limited. He needed a full-time caretaker, and I knew he was thinking: It would have been luckier to just die.

• • •

Neil V was new at the school. His family had moved to town in February. On his first day in my class, he introduced himself by saying he used to live in Virginia, but, "then some stuff happened." He was chubby and sullen and slept through most classes. Some of the other teachers said his father was abusive and his mother had had to flee their home. They were in hiding. We weren't supposed to know, but of course we knew. Neil sat by himself in the mornings before school, lounging on the grass where the killings eventually happened, earbuds jammed into his ears, and his eyes closed, his lips moving along with the song. After he died, his mother had to leave town again because her cover was blown. Neil's father saw his picture on the news just like everyone else, and he was on the way to reclaim his wife.

• • •

Laurel D was likely to be the valedictorian. She was the smartest girl the school had ever seen. She was too high-strung, I thought, to survive college, but she got high SAT scores and aced her AP tests and joined all the clubs you're supposed to join. She went to the state finals in gymnastics. Credentials don't mean anything to the bullets. They said she was the last one shot. When the shooter was chased by police out of the building, he turned back to fire at them, and a bullet ricocheted off a wall and wedged itself in Laurel's throat. Her best friend tried to close the wound with her sweater. This is how we got the most famous image of the day: Laurel's best friend, blood smeared on her face and her chest, collapsing into the arms of Laurel's boyfriend, who was covered in dust from one of the explosions. Laurel's body on a stretcher, already dead.

Both the best friend and the boyfriend would be over-whelmed with guilt for having survived and even though they were trying to live normal lives now, they were both at different colleges, knowing that the fact of their existence was a fluke.

• • •

When Hannah J was fifteen, she went on eBay and tried to sell her soul. She wanted to save up to move to Scotland and start a new life. She briefly became national news. She was a clever girl but a terrible student. She had this anger that nobody could control. Once, she flipped her desk when a teacher asked her to repeat her answer. She got in terrible fights with the other girls over the pettiest things. My mother told me that in the bleak of winter when you see your breath you're actually seeing your soul and you have to suck it back in before it escapes. For years, I tried to hold my breath while I was outside, terrified by the thought of accidentally misplacing my soul, and sometimes I would rush past strangers and try to chomp down on their vapor-ous breath to stockpile extra souls just in case. If you don't have a soul then you're just a pile of bones and muscles. I don't know who bought Hannah's soul, but I know she died without one, and when I'd asked Reverend Chet what that meant for her, he'd shrugged and said it didn't matter. He'd said souls were a myth.

• • •

Carly T was the last of the students to die. She'd spent three weeks in intensive care. Four surgeries, many pints of blood transfused. Neighbors and concerned strangers stood vigil beneath her hospital window. She ended up living for nine weeks before dying of complications related to the surgeries. The media showed her cheerleading photo while talking about her grades, her popularity, her hair. She was pretty and young and white, and people got sadder about pretty dead white girls than any other type of dead person. She was much more complex than the Small-Town Barbie they wanted her to be. She'd had a few arrests for drug misdemeanors. She and her boyfriend once stole the principal's car. Her parents were joyless and distant; her mom had chronic back pain and was overmedicated. Her dad meant well but was limited. Carly T had a blond ponytail that bounced when she jumped, and she had perfect teeth. Good teeth are enough to overcome a lot of problems. We're civilized and have developed all kinds of ways to judge the depth of another's character, but mostly we go by the show of teeth and the shine of hair and that's it. Go to the zoo and you'll see the same thing: the lion with the beautiful mane gets the lioness. The buck with the biggest antlers gets the harem of doe. It's as rational a system as any.

FEBRUARY

CALVIN WAS IN my kitchen, cooking dinner while I watched TV. He had worked as a chef for several years because restaurant work is one of those fields where being a drug addict isn't necessarily a drawback. Give a man good knives and fresh fish and suddenly he thinks he has superpowers. After rehab, Calvin had settled in to a very safe, comfortable job where he wore khakis and a polo shirt and did things with spreadsheets.

There was a time when it was very important to me to eat good and trendy food. I knew the names of the hottest restaurants. I tried the unfamiliar ingredients. I drank the recommended wine pairings. But when you live by yourself, it's hard to care about food. It's hard to motivate yourself to make a complex meal, because there is nobody to share it with. You eat the microwave dinner because it's there and you need to stay alive.

On TV, they cut to live footage of a standoff at the clock tower on Main Street. An armed militia had claimed the land and declared themselves an independent nation. "We are here to protect you," their leader, Pinckney Benedict, announced. "You do not understand it, but we are preserving your rights." Behind him, the militia held their guns in the air. One of them waved a flag. The militia members were screaming at a reporter about how the tree of liberty must be refreshed with the blood of tyrants.

"I think I would be a really good tyrant," I said.

"I've always had faith in you," Calvin said.

• • •

After dinner, we went to the clock tower to see the militia. The police had roped off a perimeter, and the captain was negotiating with Benedict via megaphone. They were nine men and one woman, plus a few bored-looking children. They wore camouflage uniforms and helmets and had amassed an impressive arsenal of weapons. The list of demands was long and unrealistic. The president would not abdicate to satisfy some angry rural people who had commandeered a useless clock tower. The police would not jail all people this group suspected of being terrorists. Mayor Randy would not deputize the militia and give them authority to police the area.

I recognized half of the militia members, even in their war costumes. Benedict was in my high school graduating class. I had slept in his house twice when I was a teenager, after parties when I was drunk and afraid of going home. He'd been nice and accommodating, and so respectful of my personal space I barely knew how to handle it. One of the younger men had mowed my lawn for three summers before moving on to college. When the cameras were off, everyone was calm. As soon as they switched to live TV, the militia started screaming and pointing their guns at the police.

The militia had assumed the public would be on their side, but everybody was making fun of them. Only one of their demands had been met: pizza delivery every afternoon, from a pizzeria that sympathized with their cause. They'd brought supplies, but not enough. At night, they camped in tents while two sentries kept watch. If anyone got within a hundred feet, they shouted warnings and pointed their guns. It was inspiring to see them at least committing to something.

◆ ◆ ◆

Calvin wanted to go to the movies. We used to go to movies with my father every weekend. My father sat by himself, in the front row, while we sat a few rows behind him. He laughed so loudly at jokes that people shushed him. During intense scenes, he leaned forward so far in his seat it looked like he was hoping to be sucked into the screen. I watched the back of his head, craned up at the screen while he shoveled popcorn into his mouth. I didn't have any idea what he loved or why. Calvin would always get up fifteen minutes into the movie, saying he had to go to the bathroom, and then sneak into a different theater. My father never knew he was gone.

"I just need to get out of the house," he said. "I want to do *something.*" I patiently explained to him the problem with movie theaters, the fact of being trapped in a darkened room with the exits so far away and easily blocked. Had he not even heard about the movie theater shooting in Fairhope? Or the one in Phoenix? There aren't any safe spaces, but there are less dangerous places. And besides, what is the point of movies? What good does watching a story about fake people do anyone?

"You're no better than them," Calvin said, pointing at the TV. The militia members were milling around aimlessly. They sometimes paced just to create a show and keep a camera on them. "The world is not out to get you."

"I never said it was." Though I thought: What if it is?

"Your paranoia makes you not even human. It just makes you this jagged shard of fear that can't do anything."

I turned off the TV and stood. If he wanted to do things, then we would do things. I put on a jacket and some shoes and told him to follow me. If we got killed, it would be on him.

. . .

I drove Calvin to the loudest restaurant in town, and then I invited Robbie to join us. I hadn't seen Robbie for two weeks, and he was getting frustrated. He texted that if I didn't get back to him soon, our relationship was over. I felt bad for him, and also I didn't want him to go away. I hadn't specifically thought about it in those terms before, but I realized it was true: I felt better with Robbie in my life than without. I was afraid to tell him that.

He didn't respond to my first text or my second, so I sent him a third: *I have a younger brother. I want you to meet him.* He was there fifteen minutes later, and ready to ask more questions than I was comfortable with. I'd asked for a table close to the open kitchen so every clang and shout would drown out our conversation. The TVs were tuned to a college basketball game. The clamor and nonsense of the basketball fans made it hard to focus for longer than a few minutes. Robbie wanted to hear stories about what I was like as a child.

"Oh Christ, I wouldn't even know where to start," Calvin said. He laughed. He laughed now more than he ever had when he was young. I wondered sometimes if he even had a right to laugh after everything he'd done and gone through. How did it not grind him down into nothing?

"Let's start with this. What did she used to do for fun?"

"It wasn't always like this," he said, looking at me while I gulped my wine. "You know what she used to do? She would take me out in the yard and play with me like we were pirates. We dug so many holes out there burying treasure."

"No," Robbie said. "There is no way she played along."

"Our dad got so pissed. We would take his stuff and bury it. One day we took this watch that I guess was worth all kinds of money. When he realized it was gone, he made us go out to dig it up, but we couldn't find it. I was supposed to make the map that time, but I must have lost it."

The restaurant was not loud enough. No place is loud enough when you want it to be.

"She was always like that," Calvin said. "That imagination, man. It was trouble."

Robbie said, "Sometimes I'm not sure whether I want to see what it's like inside her head." They laughed again. They were becoming friends. They'd been together for fifteen minutes and had already formed a bond over how I was crazy and they were not. Soon they would be staring over my shoulder at the TVs and talking about basketball. They would speak in the secret language of men bonding over nothing.

"I can't believe I've never met your brother before," Robbie said.

I pushed my menu to the center of the table. "Are we ready to order or would you rather just go home?" I said.

By the end of the meal, I was drunk. Normally, I would go back to Robbie's place, but Calvin was there to drive me home. He and Robbie did a complicated handshake hug maneuver that men seem to know automatically. I hated the idea of them being friends. On the drive, he said, "Is it like this every night?"

I reclined my seat as far as it would go.

He stopped the car in the middle of the road. He shifted into park. No one was around us. "Come on."

"How am I supposed to know what it's like?" I turned the radio back up.

"I need you to give me a real answer."

"It's been cold for a long time. You've been gone too long to understand." My breath tasted terrible. In the morning, I would hate myself. Overnight, I would wake up and try to count the drinks I'd had, try to round it down. I would start counting out the reasons I wouldn't have a drink the next day. I would map out the coming days when I would, or would not, be expected to drink, and try to determine whether I would be able to stop myself.

"Fuck," he said. He shifted into drive and pulled a U-turn.

I unbuckled my seat belt. He tried to reach over and buckle it. He was a father now, I remembered, a man who had children and took care of them. He knew how to drive safely while also reaching with one hand across the car to tend to a child. "Drive faster," I said. I wanted him to go so fast I couldn't see and then slam on the brakes and launch me through the windshield like a cartoon character in an ejector seat. I wasn't paying attention to where we were going until we were there.

He pulled into the school parking lot and turned off the lights but left the engine running. In the dark, it just looked like a normal school.

"I thought it would look worse," he said.

"The ghosts are all inside."

"After it happened, I had dreams about the school for weeks." He lit a cigarette. "It was fucked up. I hadn't even thought about this place in forever. And then every night I was dreaming I was a kid in the halls and I was so small nobody could even see me. Then the bell rang and everyone started chasing me, trying to stomp on me. I woke up before they ever got me. I didn't tell Nina about it. I just wanted it to go away." I have never known what you're supposed to say when someone tells you about a dream. "I was hoping you would call then. But you were just here getting drunk by yourself."

"If you look over there," I said, "that's where the memorial is going. By the cafeteria. It's going to be *grand*." The word felt luxurious working its way up my throat.

"I have to go home. Nina's worried about me out here with you."

$\bullet\ \bullet\ \bullet$

In Phase Two of the War on Violence, the antiviolence task force called on everyone to become "citizen journalists." The best way to catch the bad guys before the next atrocity was to record everything. Even if we didn't prevent an attack, then we could at least film the scene as it happened. The news didn't work anymore and the police didn't know how to stop the murders. When institutions fail, it's on the people to pick up the pieces or be crushed beneath the rubble. I used my phone to record everything I did.

It was hard to imagine how people had ever survived without constant surveillance. I watched other people's live streams hoping to see something, so I could then say something. All around me, people were flipping through videos of non-crimes filmed by other citizen journalists. But most people's lives, most of the time, are a long string of nothing. It is no thing then no thing again, in a row, for hours. At night, I was entranced by how dull my own days were, especially with my brother gone. Sitting in coffee shops, looking out the window for suspicious people. Walking to the post office, avoiding the cracks in the sidewalk. Exchanging money for soft drinks and sandwiches. Ordering one gin and tonic then another at Murphy's Law. Sitting in the passenger seat of Robbie's car as he drove down Main Street, past faces that were both familiar and alien.

If you caught video of a murder in progress, you could go

viral. You could get a small paycheck from the news producers. You could create content, which helped to create other content, which helped to create jobs for thousands of people. The media's appetite for video was insatiable. It needed filmed death to stay alive.

• • •

The second meeting of the Peacekeepers occurred three weeks after the first. Norm's neighbor, Charlie, joined us. Charlie was younger than Norm, and looked like the sort of man who spent his youth at rock concerts and inside dive bars. He was the kind of man who has hundreds of indistinguishable stories about high school parties. I took notes while he ran through the list of suspicious activities he'd observed in the past week. Charlie offered to drive us on our first official patrol of the neighborhood. On the rear windshield of his truck, he'd affixed more than a dozen stickers, many of them different versions of a famous comic strip character peeing on something he didn't like: Democrats, a particular football team, his ex-wife, the EPA, a soda company. Another sticker said MY FAMILY and beneath it there were four guns of various sizes, meant to represent the father gun and the mother gun and the two gun children. There was something I could respect about a man willing to so openly broadcast his anger; at least there were no secrets.

We drove for two hours, cruising slowly with our lights off so we could get the drop on criminals in the act. I sat between Charlie and Norm on the bench seat of the truck. When we turned right, I leaned into Norm and when we turned left I leaned against Charlie. Their guns slid across the dashboard on every turn, following me. You don't even need a hand to shoot someone. Guns sometimes fire themselves because they need a release. I'd read enough stories about children accidentally shooting themselves. An unexpected bump could result in two bullets to my chest.

Norm fell asleep, his face pressed against his window while he snored. Charlie rarely spoke; he chewed on an unlit cigar and changed the radio stations every couple minutes. I got into long text conversations with Robbie, pretending I was in my house, but feeling too sick to have him visit. I didn't want him to know about the Peacekeepers because I didn't think he'd understand.

◆ ◆ ◆

The Peacekeepers did their rounds two evenings a week. We never found any criminals, though we did frighten some teens who were drinking in the woods. Norm wanted to bust them so he could at least feel productive, but Charlie wanted to buy them more beer. "They could be, like, informants," Charlie said. The teens ran as soon as they saw our flashlight.

It was unclear whether our efforts mattered at all.

"What even is the fucking point of trying?" Norm said one night before he fell asleep.

"Maybe they know we're on patrol," I said. "It's like a preventative thing."

"Great, let's give the key to the city to the guy who saw nothing happening," Norm said.

"I don't even think that key works on anything," Charlie said.

• • •

The receptionist in the municipal building had worked there since I was a child. I'd known her face my whole life. A neighbor boy once told me she was a witch, two hundred years old. He told me if I ever made her angry, she would put a curse on me. I later realized this wasn't true, but still I didn't like taking chances. I rushed past her, my eyes directed at the floor, and I ignored her when she asked where I was going. I pushed through Mayor Randy's door and slammed it behind me. The way he reacted to my entrance, I realized I was the town's new witch. I was the one who would put curses on people. This was a power I'd never felt, and now I understood exactly why the witches in fairy tales would be so willing to wreck people's lives. You do it because you want people to know who you are. You put the children in an oven not because you're hungry but because you want their parents to understand the feeling of having no control. Randy retreated behind his desk and instantly looked more comfortable.

"Anna," he said, "you shouldn't just show up like this."

He gestured to an empty chair, and I sat.

"I want to talk about the memorial," I said.

"I'm afraid I can't do anything about the memorial," he said. "We've already hired a sculptor. The project is in the hands of the state now."

I couldn't understand why the state would have any say over such a thing at all.

He shrugged. "It's a hard thing to explain. Everybody wants a piece of it."

I told him my idea anyway. What I envisioned was this: no memorial at all. No stone. No American flags every three feet. No ribbons. No priests and no Bible. No symbolic floral arrangements to represent vitality or youth or rebirth. No poet reading a poem about rising from the ashes. No obelisks, for God's sake. Just dig a huge hole and fill it with guns. A hole so deep you could see the magma bubbling beneath us. Have everyone come from around the country and throw their guns into the hole. Fill it up with nitrate-rich soil. Fill it and fill it and fill it until the hole is overflowing. Then walk away. Allow the earth to process the guns and turn them into something beautiful. The earth can turn coal into diamonds; imagine what it could do with guns. Wait until the guns sprout from the ground and flower and see what new resources present themselves. After the flood, you get rainbows. After the fire, you get mushrooms. After the shooting, you just get more shootings unless you do something different.

He shuffled papers on his desk. "That's a very interesting idea," he said.

"Can I tell you how tired I am of people telling me I'm interesting?"

"I can't . . . I wouldn't even know how to begin. And what would the EPA say?"

"I think the EPA would be happy not to see more children get killed."

He dropped his head in his hands like an exasperated parent. "Look. There's a public meeting next month. Come present your idea. Do *not* say I endorsed it."

• • •

The sculptor of the memorial was a graduate student at one of the big state universities, and she looked like she was seventeen. Some days, everyone looked younger than me. I saw their faces and couldn't even imagine what it felt like to be so young. She had a crooked smile and hair that flowed past her hips. She wore clothes that didn't fit her and when people spoke to her she stared at the ground and chewed on her fingernails. Her eyes never stopped darting around her. In her tininess and frightened alertness, she reminded me, more than anything, of a bird. I watched her when she took a tour of the site, sketching ideas in her pad while the men of the town council spoke to her. I couldn't hear them because I was watching through binoculars, but I knew they were droning on about the spirit of the memorial, about closure and healing and memory. I knew she wasn't listening to them.

The next day she returned by herself to work on some sketches, so I drove to the school. I had nothing I wanted to say to her, but I also felt strongly that I needed to meet her. She did not look up from her pad when I approached. I told her my name, and it meant nothing to her. I told her I'd been falsely accused of the shooting.

"I don't pay much attention to the news," she said.

"Why are you here?"

"This is kind of a big deal for me. It's my first commissioned sculpture."

"How lucky for you that all these people died," I said.

She finally looked up from her pad. I could see she was terrified of failure. She'd chosen an impractical major in a world that holds the arts in contempt. It was an unfair thing for me to have said, but it felt good to hurt somebody. When you say something cruel, your brain releases a surge of dopamine to soothe you, and then your body starts to crave the dopamine so you become progressively meaner just to get your fix. What she was doing was pointless. It was just the next step in the playbook of a mass murder, and we needed to get through it so we could check it off the list.

"What the fuck do you want me to say to that?" she said. I hoped she would say something terribly hurtful. I wanted her to cut me so deep I would have the scar forever. Women can wound each other in ways men can never imagine. She sat down in the grass and kept sketching until I walked away.

• • •

On the ninth day of the standoff at the clock tower, one of the militia members accidentally shot himself in the foot. The sound of gunfire could have caused the police to panic, but they did not. They calmly approached and offered medical assistance. One of the militia's founding principles was to oppose government in all its forms, so they refused the help. I was in the crowd watching as they waved the ambulance off. I hated the part of me that wished someone else would fire a gun. I hated the part of me that could watch this happening and forget it was reality, wishing for terrible things to happen for the sake of my temporary entertainment.

My online therapist blocked me the day after Calvin left. She said I was being too needy. But there were plenty of other places online to bare my soul. I tried commenting on *New York Times* articles. On an article about economic sanctions on a Middle Eastern country, I wrote: "Sometimes I feel guilt for things I've never even done, and then I feel guilty for even feeling that guilt." Someone responded: "LOL." Someone else responded: "Did you even read the fucking article?"

Of course I'd read the article. What did that have to do with anything?

On an article about increased security measures at airports, I commented: "I guess I've always felt alone. I know that's why people get pets, but I'm sort of afraid if I get another cat, I'll love her too much. I'll scare her off because I'll be this concentrated beam of needy love energy. My last cat hated me so much I didn't know how to handle it." Nobody responded. On an article about rising taxes, I commented: "I feel good today. I woke up in the morning and felt lighter, smarter. I looked in the mirror and didn't hate myself. I had a good breakfast. I thought about the world and how lucky I am, relatively speaking. I want to feel like this more often." Someone responded: "wtf is wrong with you anyway?" Someone else said: "Maybe you SHOULD feel bad. Life is shitty, and you're shitty for bragging about your privilege."

Being online wasn't safe, exactly, but it was safer. Or maybe it was just dangerous in a different way. Weird little communities clustered around the most obscure interests. You could belong and not belong at the same time. Robbie said he couldn't stand the glow of the laptop in bed, so most nights I was confined to the couch. Across thousands of websites, I left comments, scraps of my personality. As if my whole life had been printed on paper, shredded, and tossed like confetti out into the wind. On car repair forums, there were notes about my brief period as a high school field hockey player. On fashion blogs, there were snippets about my junior prom. On the box scores of basketball games, there were descriptions of freshman dorm life. "Haven't you heard of identity theft?" Robbie said. "Why can't you just get a journal?"

The thought of compiling it all in one place was dreadful. Being able to pick and choose when and where information was distributed, being able to control the story by scattering it: that was the only responsible approach.

• • •

With Calvin back home with his family, I suspected he was texting Robbie behind my back, and I suspected Robbie of spying on me. He was relentless in trying to get me some kind of help. He signed me up for two different support groups: one for survivors of trauma and one for depressives. In the morning, he woke me and coaxed me through getting showered and getting dressed, and then he made me lunch, and when I asked where he was taking me, he said, "You don't get to ask questions. This is nonnegotiable." When we arrived at the local Methodist church, I worried he was taking me to get baptized. I'd been baptized as a child, and it had done nothing to help me. Robbie had called Renee and asked her to chaperone me, so she was standing at the door of the church. She needed help as much as I did. I didn't even know Robbie had her phone number.

He was prepared to chase me down if I tried to escape. But the truth is, once I passed through the front door of the church, the most difficult part was over. When I looked over at him, the hard set of his jaw, the defiant look in his eyes, I thought for the first time that I might love him.

I didn't love him, but right then I felt like I did. I was impressed by him. I acted like I hated him for it. I thought he might feel cheated if I went easily. This was a heroic moment for Robbie. I thought it would be cruel to ruin it by making it too easy.

The group, fifteen people including me and Renee, met three times weekly. Nobody asked me about the shooting unless I brought it up. Nobody ever accused me of anything. Mostly, what I did was sit and listen and sometimes cry. It's a paradox that surrounding yourself with more misery helps you to feel better. If you can't breathe, the best thing you can do is sink yourself deeper into the sea and wait until you grow gills. That's just evolution. Here, everyone understood the fear and I was able to tell them that every day I felt afraid. Every day, the act of leaving my house felt audacious. Even in a church basement, I worried I might be the victim of an elaborate trap. And what they did, every time, was let me talk. When I left the meetings, Robbie was waiting in his car to pick me up.

Jenna O spoke to our support group one evening. She had been shot three times at the school, and lost so much blood that they didn't think she would ever regain consciousness. She awoke from her coma after a week. She'd lost the use of her legs. She would undergo ten surgeries in the first five months to try to ameliorate the damage to the nerves in her hands, the scarring on her face. She would look like a victim for the rest of her life. Had I been her, I would have gone into hiding. But she kept speaking. She appeared on the news, and she took the podium at the many vigils and rallies. She became a spokeswoman for the anti-gun movement. Sometimes she received threats from people who were very concerned about how her disfigurement might inconvenience them. The surgeries had fixed her face in an expression of permanent disgust. She had been a weak student, distracted and immature, but now she was a different person. During one speech, she spoke compassionately about the boy himself. "I've read everything he's ever written," she said, "and it breaks my heart to know that he was so unhappy and we were *right there*. We're surrounded by people like him, and we need to stop pretending everything is fine."

In the church basement, she told us she knew how hard it was to overcome the fear and the sadness, but that we had a moral responsibility to do so. Sometimes she had to pause because her brain didn't quite move at the speed it used to. Sometimes she slurred her speech. She kept saying, "Everything happens for a reason," as if this fact had ever been in doubt. Then she listened. I felt ashamed to be sitting in the same room as her. I felt unentitled to my own emotions. I felt like a failure for having even had any negative thoughts about life when mine was much better than so many other people's. Everyone wanted me to get better, which meant they wanted me to stop being sad, but being sad was the only thing I needed. The real problem is when people flinch from the sadness and hide. Men see a sad woman and they want to fix her, but in fixing her they flatten her emotional life under the weight of meaningless platitudes. I left the room and Renee did not follow. Robbie was not there yet. I ran.

I was embarrassed to go home and tell Robbie I'd left the meeting. I was sick of explaining myself. I picked up two bottles of Crown Royal and walked to the clock tower. I thought the militia guys might get a laugh out of the crown thing, since they were so opposed to monarchy, but they didn't even think about it. Pinckney Benedict frisked me and then opened the bottle. "Did you bring any cups?" he said.

They were overall an uninteresting group of drinking buddies. They didn't want to have conversation; they just wanted to lodge grievances. I would have been better off sitting in newspaper comments sections, because at least I could have closed the tab when I was done. At this point, the militia was very weak. The children had long ago lost interest in playing army. The man who'd shot himself in the foot was in incredible pain and kept saying they were going to have to amputate his foot. "I'm sorry you think liberty is worth less than your damn foot, Gary," Benedict said.

"You said we'd be done here in a week," Gary said. "And I'm out here dying like an asshole."

Benedict called everyone into formation for the shooting of their daily video. He asked me to hold the camera, because their tripod was broken. He addressed their followers, and asked for supplies. "This is George Washington in Valley Forge time," he said. The winter cold without a sun was enough to kill you. The heat lamps did very little to help. "This is a chance for a true patriot to save us." I wondered how many people were skeptical of Washington and Jefferson and the others when they were out making trouble for everyone. I wondered if I would have been on the right side of history if I'd lived then.

Benedict's son was a precocious, angry little boy. He had a seemingly endless supply of rocks to throw at nearby businesses. His name was Constitution. "You'd never see the president name a kid Constitution, would you?" Benedict said. I agreed he probably would not do such a thing. I found it easiest to agree and agree until I was too drunk to really listen.

Without sunlight, it was hard to tell if it was morning, but the others were already milling around, trying to look soldierly, while I rolled out of my hungover sleep. The media had gotten bored days ago and some had already left town, but there were a few cameramen on site. It was going to be bad for me if anyone recognized me standing in the so-called freedom circle. I turtled my head into my sweater and scrambled away from the scene, knowing it was already too late. A state trooper cuffed me before I reached the sidewalk. On the news, there was footage of me, pressed to the ground, an officer's knee in my back. "Former shooting suspect arrested," they said.

• • •

Robbie had to bail me out. They cited me for disorderly conduct, public intoxication, and three other quality-of-life crimes I don't remember. I faced a court date and owed a $3,000 fine. I did not have $3,000. The unemployment had lasted six months and my savings were almost gone. Calvin was still sending me checks, but I was not cashing them. At that point, I was unemployable. My face and name had been connected to a school shooting, and now another arrest. My choices in this town were limited and unpleasant. The only real choice I had was to leave.

I'd gotten used to Robbie looking at me like a disappointed parent, but as he led me out of the station, hand gripped hard around my elbow, he seethed. He released me when we got to his car. "I'll give you a ride, but you can't come to my place," he said. He still looked so young, but in his eyes and in the patch of gray stubble on his chin, I saw his future. I saw him with close-cropped hair and business casual attire, his sleeves rolled up precisely to his elbows as he sat down for a happy-hour drink with a client. I saw him wearing shoes instead of flip-flops. I saw him talking to the client about his new dog and his new baby, and how it's been a little crazy, yeah, but we're adjusting, we're surviving. I saw him yawning at five thirty and then heading home, walking instead of driving because he'd had two drinks and anyway it's a nice night out and he could use the fresh air. I saw him entering his home and seeing his wife feeding the baby, and then running around in the yard with the puppy for a few minutes before giving his wife a break. I saw him cleaning the baby's face and then tossing it casually up in the air several times and smiling, and then later laying the baby down into bed. I saw him fifteen years later, holding his daughter's hand and telling her he was proud of her and trusted her, but please let him know if the new boyfriend ever gets fresh with her. I saw his whole life flashing before my eyes and I knew: he was going to turn out to be a very good man. He already was a good man. I was not part of his future.

"If you're going to get in the car, just get in the car," he said. He couldn't even make eye contact. I had him drop me off at Murphy's Law. I knew once I got out I wouldn't see him again, and I had no idea what I was supposed to do to change that.

MARCH

ONE DAY the confession booth was replaced by a mailbox-shaped robot. The robot had a message written on its chest: you are being watched for your safety. It swiveled in a full circle periodically, but never left that corner. Seldom Falls had been chosen as the recipient of one of the first public security robots in the nation. This was a pilot of a program called SENTRY (Safety Ensured Nationally Through Robotic Yeomen). "Where did the booth go?" I asked the robot.

"I can only answer questions about safety," the robot said.

"You must get lonely out here."

"This does not appear to be a safety-related question."

"Do you have a girlfriend?"

"Warning sign: erratic behavior. Please report to hospital for evaluation."

I did not like the attitude of this robot.

• • •

At the high school, they conducted random locker checks for contraband weapons, and students who were categorized as aggressive were quarantined in classrooms where they couldn't disturb the other students. As part of a program called Never Again, they spent Friday mornings quietly reflecting on the sadness of violence. Students had to sign a pledge vowing to defend their peers against all attackers. They held shelter-in-place drills, during which they practiced being shot at, but safely. After two months, nobody had been shot. Our state senator's approval ratings were higher than they had ever been. He pushed for this school safety plan to be adopted statewide. But, before these policies, we had previously gone many decades without a shooting. Some people confuse good luck with strategy.

• • •

After a car bomb in San Francisco killed seven and injured a dozen others, the country went on high alert for terrorist attacks. It was impossible for me to ramp up my vigilance further, but I tried. I texted Calvin to ask if he was okay and he said he was fine. "lol why the hell would terrorists attack seldom falls?" he said. "Like you could even tell if someone set off a bomb there." Terrorists liked to attack places of financial or symbolic value, and Seldom Falls was neither. It made sense not to worry about it. But it also made sense to look for terrorists everywhere, to continue recording every step I took, just in case. If the attacks were predictable, then nobody would ever be killed by them. People wanted to treat the violence like the weather; it was there, inevitably, and they felt that with enough advanced equipment they could predict where it would strike next. The possibility of the violence not existing had not occurred to anyone.

• • •

When I was young, before my brother lived with us, there was a rash of small bombings around the country. I wasn't supposed to know about it; adults assume kids don't pay attention to the news, and maybe some don't, but after my father left for work, I sat at the table with a newspaper spread in front of me. I liked highlighting words I didn't understand. I liked both knowing and not really knowing. The police said it was a loner, planting bombs in objects that looked like debris. He would leave something that looked like a wood scrap in a parking lot, and when someone bent to move that wood scrap it would explode. For months, I lived in fear of normal objects. What I feared most were things that didn't look like bombs, because those were most likely to be bombs. My mother told me I couldn't live my whole life afraid of everything. Now I understand that most advice people give is actually directed at themselves. My father spent nights with me, walking through the neighborhood cautiously, classifying items as bombs, non-bombs, or bombs disguised as non-bombs. Once we identified a safe object, he would walk up to it and touch it first, and then I would touch it too. We never blew up. If we found a bomb, my father wrote the exact location in his notepad and promised to call the police when we got home. One night, he spotted a strange, unmarked box on the curb. I was certain this was the bomb that would explode us, and I held on to his shirt telling him we had to go right away, but he kept walking, and as he approached it, I ducked, because at school my teacher had told us explosions move upward, like heat. I started crying because I knew my father was about to die. He touched the box and shook it, and then lifted it over his head like a circus strongman. He'd dropped his flashlight in the grass, and so from my vantage point, I saw his legs illuminated and a dark place where his face was. The box was full of old golf trophies. My father shook the box around and I felt reassured then. Not everything explodes. Most things don't.

♦ ♦ ♦

I was twenty-four when he killed himself. He stood up early from Easter dinner without a word, walked out into the backyard, sat down on a tree stump, put a shotgun in his mouth, and pulled the trigger. We heard the sound, and Calvin was the one who saw him first. He was only sixteen, and had been home from rehab for a month. He would overdose for the second time that night. I saw my father's ghost, strolling around in the backyard as if nothing had happened. His ghost is gone now. I used to see it back there when I drove by, but a few years ago, it dematerialized. The night of my father's second death, I cried so violently, I thought it would detach the ligaments from my bones.

♦ ♦ ♦

The public meeting about the memorial opened by wasting time on various state officials taking their share of the credit for the planning of this event, and municipal officials soliciting donations. "If we could do this for free," a councilman said, "we would. But listen, things are not free. If we just gave memorials away, everyone would want one." This was followed by several speeches about the importance of properly honoring the dead. Everyone wanted their chance to announce exactly how the shooting had affected them.

When finally I had the opportunity to speak, I made the same suggestion I'd made to Randy last month. I knew before I finished my first sentence that they wouldn't listen to me. I continued anyway. I said a memorial's greatest value is in show-ing us how to avoid this kind of tragedy in the future. I said that what we really needed was a mural of all the police looking the other way while that boy strolled by armed with the arsenal of a small army. "People died because of you," I said. "You let this happen." I hadn't planned on saying that. Most of my thoughts spend very little time in my head before they make themselves known. Sometimes I don't realize my thoughts are mine until I hear them.

I felt the hands of security guards on my shoulders, and I had to make a choice: leave calmly and with my dignity, or continue shouting as they dragged me away.

Dignity is overrated.

◆ ◆ ◆

Given enough time and enough tragedies, we will eventually run out of places for new memorials. Every square inch of the planet will be covered by plaques commemorating a war or a shooting or a building collapse or a massive fire. We will be reminded of the inevitability of tragedy, but when you try to make it impossible to forget, then there is no point in remembering.

• • •

Angie and Reverend Chet stopped at my house. "We decided to give you one more chance," Angie said. Reverend Chet entered my home without my permission and unrolled blueprints on my table. They explained that I was seeing the blueprints for an apocalypse bunker, already in construction deep in the woods an hour from here. They needed my help. My labor, primarily, but also donations. Canned goods, bottled water, blankets, fitness equipment. Chet showed me the blueprint. I pretended I understood how to read blueprints. "It looks good," I said. It was one of the best-designed apocalypse bunkers I'd ever seen. They said they had a master carpenter building out the walls now. I did not envy her job. To be a carpenter for a Christian church is a significant burden, considering the lineage.

For the bunker to work, God would need to launch an apocalypse, but forget to look underground for survivors. The Old Testament God was a foul-tempered teenage boy. He was a C student, constantly being tricked and distracted and outwitted. He'd forget about his creation for millennia and then come back to it looking to take out his hormonal rage. Chet was a big believer in this god.

"This seems like the sort of thing a cult would do," I said.

Angie looked at me like I'd just said something very stupid. "Well, yes. Of course it is."

"The idea that all cults are bad is a myth brought to you by

Uncle Sam," Reverend Chet said. "Jesus himself was considered a cult leader in his day."

"But they killed Jesus," I said.

"And they'll kill us too if we let them," he said. "To be classified as a cult would be an honor."

The idea of hiding underground for a few years until everything got better was appealing. That's why groundhogs look so happy.

"Can I have a few days to think about it?" I said.

Angie laughed at me. "No, honey. No," she said. "You've proven yourself untrustworthy. We're just here for donations."

I gave them a few cans of soup, and they left.

Reverend Chet had preached to us once that if we truly believed, and we committed to taking action, then we would be just like Noah. I didn't want to be Noah. Noah was a bad person. Noah was a coward. He should have listened to God and then told him: No. I like it here. You don't get to kill everyone just because you screwed up. Instead he abandoned them all and floated away to safety with his menagerie of giraffes and walruses. Noah had to build an ark because God decided to kill everyone on Earth, and then later God apologized with a rainbow. It doesn't add up. The apology does not have the same weight as the bodies.

◆ ◆ ◆

A group of teenagers used a live stream to record themselves raping a girl at a party. A man in Little Rock went on a killing spree and streamed every murder, as revenge on the woman who had recently divorced him. He broke into the homes of senior citizens and made them kneel on the floor. He made them beg, made then say the name of his ex-wife. Then he shot them and looked into the camera and said, "This is your fault." I tried not to watch the killings, but everywhere around me there were screens. In line at the bakery, I heard a man shouting and looked just in time to see the video playing on the phone of the teenager in front of me. He and his friends watched the murder over and over with a dead-eyed curiosity, the way they would view any other piece of viral content.

Anything can be entertainment if you watch it enough. The value of your life is directly proportionate to the number of ads they can run before the video of your murder. This particular murder had garnered over a million views, so it had been a very good one indeed. I tapped the teenager on the shoulder and asked him to turn his phone off. He looked up at me and smiled, then he made a motion with his hand like he was jerking off. He turned his phone off, but he and his friends laughed at me. I stayed in line because I'd wanted to buy fresh bread and I didn't want to give these children the satisfaction of walking away.

◆ ◆ ◆

When I was ten, the Desperate Father knocked on my door after sunset and told me he wanted to go on an adventure. He was wearing a heavy backpack and a jacket he'd bought at the army surplus store. He hadn't showered in days. "Get your things together. We have a mission tonight," he said. The backseat of his car was piled with trash from fast-food restaurants. Styrofoam clamshells open and flapping like their throats had been slit. He blindfolded me—I trusted him, I didn't question being blindfolded—and said, "I can't have you knowing the route, in case we get captured." I didn't understand what that meant.

A half hour into the drive, I said, "I have school tomorrow."

"Oh, I'm sorry to take you on an adventure. Why would I ever think my own daughter would want to join her father on an adventure? What an idiot I am for thinking my own daughter, who always complains about being bored, would want to do something exciting."

When we parked, finally, he removed my blindfold. "There are werewolves out here," he said, running his finger along a road in a hand-drawn map. "They nest out in this area, where I drew the little star."

The moon was full. We were in a wooded area I didn't recognize. For the first time in my life, I thought: I think Dad is crazy. I thought: He wasn't always crazy. Now I don't know if I was right or if he was just sad, or if there's even a difference. Everyone knows about mental illness, but nobody really thinks it's going to affect them.

He led me through the woods, telling me he'd gotten a hot tip from a friend on this werewolf nest, and if we found them, then we could capture them and maybe even kill them. "Then you won't have to have your nightmares anymore," he'd said. It was a hopeful thought, but I didn't believe it. I didn't think we would find werewolves. I also didn't think there was such a thing as a cure for nightmares. Along the perimeter of the woods, I saw some lights, trailers with families in them. I worried that one of my classmates would see me with my father, who was clutching a knife and calling out directions while I followed with a flashlight. If we did find a nest, would I even have been able to kill a werewolf? What if one of them was a puppy? What if it looked me in the eyes and demanded an explanation?

I kept walking through spiderwebs. I felt covered in bugs. We caught nothing. We drove home and I fell asleep, and the nightmares did not go away.

◆ ◆ ◆

My mother insisted on hosting Easter dinner even after my father's suicide. During the next three years, Calvin sneaked away from the table repeatedly to snort cocaine in the bathroom and then we pretended we didn't know he was high. The fourth year, he missed dinner because he was serving a six-month sentence for assault. The fifth year, he was in rehab, and on the sixth he refused to come because his counselor had told him the house was toxic. I sat with my mother at the table. She asked me to say grace, and I refused. I was beyond trying to believe in any particular god. I was beyond ham and potatoes. We had each brought a bottle of wine, and drank straight from our respective bottles. She left seats open for my father and my brother, because she was hoping for a resurrection. "Do you know how hard I've worked in my life?" she said. "Are you aware of the sacrifices a woman has to make in order to be a mother? Do you know what love is worth? It is worth nothing."

"I think I'll go home," I said.

"Stay and eat. I don't even like ham."

"Nobody likes ham. It's made out of pigs."

"Do you plan on having a future?" She swirled her wine. She had recently taken classes on wine appreciation, and now she swirled everything she drank vigorously, like she was mixing paint. "Or is this who you intend to be for the rest of your life?"

"Did you ever think we could turn out to be friends?" I asked.

"I tried very hard to be a good mother. I gave you the things you needed. You're the first person in the family to graduate college. You may as well have gone to the moon."

Later, we threw the ham in the trash. I helped her up the stairs to her bed. She died before the next Easter. She had a heart attack overnight and nobody was there to help her. I spoke at her funeral and said many things about how she was loving and warm and kind and funny, and it's hard to say whether I was lying then or if I'm lying now.

HOW TO BE SAFE, PART III

SPEND A YEAR burrowing deep into your backyard and developing a network of complex tunnels as both escape routes and your new home. If you don't have a backyard, then choose a remote area of a public park or nature preserve. Get used to eating grubs and dirt. Prepare yourself for turf wars with gophers and naked mole rats and prairie dogs. Sometimes eat a prairie dog for protein and to establish dominance. Never, ever come up for air.

SLEEP WITH A KNIFE under your pillow. Make sure it's a serrated knife, with at least a six-inch blade, sharpened. Make sure it's a knife that has a taste for blood and is greedy for more. A knife that will cut someone even if you're reluctant, that will push through your fear and into the flesh of your attacker. Attach the knife to a gun. Attach yourself to the gun and turn yourself into a bayonet. Be willing to dive into the trenches and disembowel somebody if necessary.

AT NIGHT, when you're alone in the relative safety of your home— assuming the electricity and plumbing are up to code, assuming there are no major natural disasters on the horizon, assuming there are no psychopaths or escaped convicts lurking outside and waiting to see your bedroom light flick off before they climb in through your window—listen to your heartbeat and take a few deep breaths and consider that with each inhalation you are ingesting thousands of harmful microbes and think about what it looks like inside of you, what it sounds like, how it would feel to live inside your own self. Understand that anything you do to protect yourself is temporary and pointless, but also that you have no choice but to keep doing it. Reassess your motivations. Reach out for someone to sit beside you in terror and longing and share that quiet moment with that person, understanding this may be the last one you have.

APRIL

Two weeks before the anniversary and the unveiling of the memorial, the militia ended their occupation. They released a statement claiming they'd made their point by drawing the nation's attention to their cause. They promised to continue fighting against government tyranny. But they read it with little conviction. They were a tired, huddled mass of disappointed men. They packed up. Most revolutions don't end in bloodshed; they just end.

The national media returned to Seldom Falls soon after. They would call this the final chapter of our story, because our attention span for atrocities is fleeting. They still told stories about redemption and the power of a town overcoming grief. They kept saying we were a phoenix rising from the ashes. Nobody even knows what a phoenix is, but everyone wants to be one. They knocked on my door and they kept knocking, while inside I was packing. I was not a phoenix; I was just a person who wished she lived in an era when people could still disappear.

• • •

They say the Earth is so big but when you want to hide, you can't. They show you the globe spinning in space, and yet there you are, all the time, in front of everyone. You are perpetually found, or in danger of being found. The only way to be invisible is to be so poor, or so sick, that nobody wants to see you. You're either seen or not seen and you have no say over it. I'd thought the easiest place for me to hide would be in the husk of my old life. I had built a life insulated from my past, but your past doesn't vanish. It's always waiting for you to come back to it. Calvin was here again, and I couldn't keep pretending it was possible to exist only in the present.

He wanted to be there for the memorial. And he said he'd heard from Robbie about my problems. I didn't like friendships branching off of me like this, the weight of them dragging me down even though I had no control over them. I explained to Calvin that I didn't need support, what I needed was a way out.

"Why don't you come and live with me?" he said. "It has to be better than this."

I couldn't live with him. He had the dog. He had a wife. He had two healthy, cheerful, imaginative children. "What would I even do there?" I said.

"I mean, what do you do here? You've never had any hobbies. You don't know anybody."

My mother always warned me that idle people are uninteresting, that men don't marry women without interests or skills.

My father, in the early days, defended me. "She's going to be an artist," he'd tell my mother. "She's living the life of the mind."

I had tried many hobbies. I tried becoming interested in theatre, but I got bored. I tried painting, but the only thing I could reasonably reproduce was a horse. Nobody needs to look at horses that badly. I tried gardening, but I couldn't keep anything alive. I tried crossword puzzles and I tried jogging and I tried photography and I tried push-ups and I tried religion. I was tired of people saying I had not tried.

"What I'm saying," Calvin said, "is you need to make room in your life for positive things." I don't remember him ever smiling as a boy. I can't even prove he had teeth then. He was a sour, sulking boy, and then he was a victim, and then he was angry. Even when he thought something was funny, his laughter was like an angry bark. He pounded his fists on tables to indicate his approval. He'd had no room in his life for positive things. And now as an adult he was a smiling, handsome, and generous man. "You can't build a life entirely around misery," he said.

• • •

The father of Paul S killed himself days before the anniversary. He streamed it live online, because he said he wanted people to see exactly the damage a gun does when it's pressed against someone's skull. He wanted to become a martyr. But his son was already a martyr, and the sad thing about martyrs is that they don't matter. They're just dead bodies. After his son's death, he had become an advocate for gun restrictions. He was angry, and

219

handsome, and intelligent, and his anger only made him more photogenic. On the Internet, they claimed he'd never even had a son, that he was an actor hired by the government as part of an anti-gun conspiracy. They told him his son was not dead. They said it often enough that I almost believed them. But it had happened. I know it did, because I saw bodies. I saw the coffins. I saw the sun dive into the lake. I'd been breathing this atmosphere full of death for almost a year. I know what it tastes like. I know the feel of it on my skin.

• • •

At the memorial service, I stood in the back of the crowd with Calvin. We were in the end zone of the football field. I didn't want to be seen and I didn't really want to see. Nearly everyone I knew was there—neighbors, former students, former friends, former coworkers, grocery store cashiers, mechanics. I scanned the crowd looking for Renee, for Robbie, but I knew Renee would be too afraid and Robbie would prefer to watch on TV. I hoped he would see my face on camera and for a minute have to think something nice about me.

The militia clustered in front of the stage holding signs about liberty and tyranny. Security was intense: metal detectors, no bags allowed at all, wheelchairs checked for contraband, bomb-sniffing dogs circulating through the crowd, snipers on the roof of the school. Drones circled overhead. Norm and Charlie patrolled the perimeter wearing shirts that said YOU ARE BEING PROTECTED BY THE PEACEKEEPERS. Charlie waved to me when he saw me. There was more security here than there had ever been for any event in the history of Seldom Falls. And yet I thought: If someone wanted to, they could kill a lot of people here. It happens all the time.

◆ ◆ ◆

A large white van pulled up in the parking lot. Angie and some other members of the church spilled out. They were distributing pamphlets about their bunker, and their need for donations. Angie handed one to me and one to Calvin.

She told me it was 80 percent complete. "We need more support if we're going to finish it," she said. She looked at me as if she'd just remembered who I was. "You've already thrown away your opportunity to be saved."

I turned to Calvin. "Do you see what happens when I try a new hobby?"

He skimmed the pamphlet. "You're friends with my sister?" he said.

"Your sister isn't interested in being a friend." Someone tapped on the microphone for a sound check. The crowd's murmuring grew louder. The buzz of drones overhead a constant reminder of electric death.

On the other side of the field, there was a sudden uproar and a shout, and then someone fired a flare gun straight up in the air. Angie took two steps away from us, widened her stance, and fired her own flare. Four flares hissed above us and flashed bright in the artificial daylight, and then fizzled out. There was a terrible panic and in the commotion, Reverend Chet charged the stage to shout that he had room for the saved, if only they would follow him, but before he finished, he was tackled and shocked with a Taser, and Angie was scrambling away, and everywhere there were people rushing to be heroes and subdue the attackers. In the chaos, I sank to my knees and buried my head in my hands, and everywhere there was panic and everywhere there was no control over anything, and all I'd ever wanted was control of *one thing* and as I sat there trying to block out the noise I kept thinking: If I stand up right now and do something, I will have control. I saw a dozen versions of myself filtering through the crowd, some of them trying to restrain the culprits while others tried to free them, some of them leading people in prayer, some of them simply leaving. Somewhere in there, the real version of me ended up chasing Angie and tackling her and holding her down until the police came. Calvin pulled me up to my feet and wrapped his arm around my shoulder and he held on to me and I knew that he was a good man, and that was miraculous enough.

It took forty-five minutes to calm everyone down. Some people left. But Calvin and I stayed. The church members had presented no real threat to the crowd, but their plan had been spectacularly ill considered. The militia stayed put, but now surrounded by armed guards, they were silent. The state would kill them if necessary to make this ceremony go on. Eventually, the mayor took the stage to introduce the governor, who introduced the corporate titan who had funded the art. The corporate titan asked the artist to unveil the memorial. It looked like a memorial. People cried, but the stone didn't matter. The bodies mattered. The blood in the soil mattered. I didn't know what they could do to make it mean something more. People applauded. Cameras flashed.

After a moment of silence, followed by the performance of the national anthem, followed by the peaceful firing of military rifles, we were expected to feel that the misery had been erased. The mayor took the stage to make another announcement. Closure had occurred.

During his previous visit, I had asked Calvin what he prayed about at night, and if he ever worried about his prayers ending up in the wrong hands. "I just pray about people. That they be okay," he'd said. "I pray for Harlan especially." His son was four years old. He was no longer in the house all day and was therefore less safe than he'd ever been. "I tell God that if anyone ever hurts Harlan, I'm going to start killing people and never stop."

On his last day with me, Calvin pulled something out of his bag and said, "I found this at my place, in an old box." It was one of our treasure maps from years ago. My handwriting, my outline of the old house, with a little rhyme I'd written at the top to hint at what treasure had been hidden. The ink was faded; the hint was unreadable. But knowing the style of my maps, we were both able to scan it and know roughly that something had been hidden in the far corner of the backyard, behind the tall maple that used to stand guard over our house.

I drove us toward the old house while Calvin closed his eyes and practiced deep-breathing exercises. I wasn't sure why he would suggest going back to this place. I told him about the tree being cut down after a bad summer storm. I told him that one of the victims had lived here, and that the family had sold the house and moved far away. I didn't know the person who lived here now, but he looked happy enough. "It wasn't the house's fault," I said. It was a dumb thing to say. But sometimes it's better to say a dumb thing than to sit in silence.

The owner wasn't home. I peeked in the windows. Inside, they'd changed everything. The walls were painted in bold reds and blues. The carpet had been torn up and replaced by hardwood. It was a different house entirely. The Earth shifts beneath our feet and turns imperceptibly into a new planet every day, and yet it's still the same place we remember. Calvin was waiting in the car with the shovels. He didn't want to get out until he had to. "It's hard to explain," he said. "Just looking at the place messes me up." There's nothing rational about most fears, but there's no turning them off. My rational brain can read all the statistics and positive outlooks, but my body knows that it can be destroyed in seconds. The brain and the body don't have the same goals. They don't have the same understanding of the world.

We dug a hole, and then we dug another hole. The ground had been frozen solid for so long that it took all of my strength just to cut into it. We were guessing about the exact location of the treasure. Would it be deeper underground than when we had buried it? What even was it? Had we dug it up before, years ago? It was possible Calvin had already found this treasure and pawned it years ago.

Every time a car rumbled down the street, I froze, trying to think how I would explain myself if we were caught. We dug a dozen shallow holes. I hit something hard, but it was just a tree root. "There's probably nothing here," I said.

He started another hole. So I started another hole. My hands were blistering. Sweat dripped into my eyes and I thought about the flesh ripping off my palms with each swipe. My back was sore and weak.

"Shit," he said. He stopped and rested his chin on the handle of the shovel. "I don't know what I thought would happen."

Until then, I'd held out the slimmest hope that I would find some relic of my father. I held out hope that there would be one item in that yard that would perfectly explain everything. A loose screw that had fallen out of me and could now be replaced, tightened, and set me back to normal. Calvin dropped his shovel and wrapped me in a hug. His shirt was transparent from the sweat. Treasure isn't the point of the hunt. The point is making the holes and sweating the sweat. While he held me I hoped my nose wouldn't bleed on his shirt.

◆ ◆ ◆

It had been a year since the sun had gone missing, and so Seldom Falls abandoned the search. It was gone and there was no way they could reapply it to the sky. Within a week, they would be unveiling an artificial sun—an incredible structure in the center of town that must have cost hundreds of millions of dollars. It used "space-age technology." I didn't really understand how it would work, but Mayor Randy promised it would be a permanent solution for "our sun problem." In fact, we would have more control than ever over our seasons. "It's a new day for Seldom Falls," he said. "This represents man's triumph over the fickle heart of nature."

After a while you get used to it all. At first, the artificial sun doesn't feel right, the color is off, the intensity of the rays isn't quite what you expect, but it's a close enough approximation. You remember the sun, but not really. Every now and then someone suggests finding a way to bring it back, but it's hard to imagine anymore why you needed it in the first place. In a decade, it will be hard to believe you even relied on the sun for anything. In Seldom Falls, they'll laugh about how people used to get skin cancer from standing in the sun for too long. Getting used to it is what kills you, but it happens.

The only thing tying me to Seldom Falls was a masochistic nostalgia, the comfort of being surrounded by familiar traumas. Calvin had returned to his family. I wasn't going to stay with him. But I was going to move near him. I was going to be somewhere where I could see him and he could see me. It would be good for us.

♦ ♦ ♦

Where I live now doesn't matter. I live in a place with a door that locks and walls the color of a cooked crab. In the morning I water plants, and in the evening I shower, and between, I do many things. I drink sometimes. I'm trying to do it less. I help people, sometimes. I lurch forward, sometimes against my will, and I feel not quite whole but not quite broken.

I saw Robbie twice before I left. The first time, he didn't

know I was seeing him. I watched him sit in a coffee shop and read the paper, smearing little bits of newspaper ink on his face. I felt a maternal urge to wet my finger and wipe it off his cheek. He sipped his coffee and he checked his phone, and he never looked over his shoulder or worried that the people in the room might hate him. I wanted to be his coffee and sit there in his mug getting colder while he was distracted by a fly buzzing around him, and then I wanted to be swallowed in one hasty gulp before he stood up to leave.

The second time, we were both in line at my mother's old deli on a busy Saturday afternoon. I took a number and his number was lower than mine. I remembered being young and spending hours pulling the numbers out of that machine, their predictability a comfort. There was a day when I pulled and I pulled, watching the numbers rise sequentially until I pulled on the seventy and out came a fourteen. I pulled again and then got a sixty-two. I worried that something had broken in my brain and I could no longer read numbers, and then when the sequence reset itself, I remember thinking you can't count on anything to make sense, not even numbers.

Robbie stood beside me, and he nodded.

"I'm leaving," I told him.

He stared deep into the case of meats as if trying to decipher the mysteries of ham.

"I need to be somewhere else."

"You still have some stuff in my apartment," he said. He stepped up to the counter and ordered.

Fifty percent of all relationships end at deli counters. Ten percent of all relationships end with a terrible argument in front of strangers at a car wash. Five percent end amicably. Two percent end in murder. Twelve percent were with the right person at the wrong time. Sixteen percent end because one person is too serious for the other. Four percent end at the dinner table because one person slurps their food and chews with their mouth open and the other one finally snaps and says, *If you don't stop chewing with your mouth open I'm going to stab you with this knife* and the other person says, *Fine go ahead and stab me I don't care*. Zero point one percent are between people named Anna and Robbie, and they are doomed to failure because ninety-nine percent of people named Anna don't know how to appreciate the good things they have.

On my last night in my old life, I had a dream that I was surrounded by guns. Every piece of furniture in my apartment had transformed into a gun and every person I knew had become a gun, and the only non-gun in the world was me. There were triggers everywhere. One misstep would lead to the firing of a gun and a chain reaction of other triggers until at some point bullets were screaming past me in all directions. I ran, zigzagging, hoping to force myself into the path of a bullet, but nothing ever touched me, and the more I ran, the more guns fired. My ears and bones were ringing, and in all the explosions I felt myself being pulled apart, my molecules stretched and twisted in every direction. Before I woke up, I had been scattered into a million pieces and spread across half the state.

◆ ◆ ◆

I drove across the border with a few bags in my trunk and a thermos full of coffee. I was going to go to a place where nobody in the world besides my brother had ever known me. I wanted to be a woman who wore cute dresses to community events and who smiled at strangers not out of fear but out of friendliness. I wanted to be a coworker whom people could trust to get the job done. I wanted to be someone who baked cakes for neighbors on their birthdays.

On the highway, I remembered long drives with my mother and my father, their silence in the front while I flipped through old issues of *National Geographic* or played card games with myself. I remembered the sound of cars hurtling past and the static of the oldies radio station as we drove out of range. I remembered the sudden reemergence of new radio stations through the static, the sign that we'd found our way back into civilization. In the backseat of the car, I was not in control of where I was going, but I was hopeful. I didn't know about most bad things yet. I tried now, as the driver, to feel the same way, and to be someone who looks forward to things. I read the signs and the billboards, and I tried to open myself to the possibilities of being alive. I thought about the ways people can be fulfilled and I reminded myself they are not faking it, they are actually happy, people can actually be happy, they are people who go outside and act on the world and let it act on them and they feel okay about it all. I wanted to be one of those people, and I didn't know how I could be that, but that's where I was headed. What I wanted, more than anything, was to be somewhere where I felt safe enough to try again.

ACKNOWLEDGMENTS

I owe gratitude to hundreds of people. I hope the people I don't list here will understand the limitations of both text space and human memory, and further understand that I am indebted to them all.

My wife, LauraBeth, is my first reader and my best friend, and if not for her, I wouldn't have the courage to even try writing books.

Every person I meet in publishing goes out of their way to tell me that my agent, Julie Barer, is the best agent in the world, and, if anything, they're selling her short.

My editor, Katie Adams, pushed me to cut all the fat out of this book, and gave me permission to take the story where it really needed to go.

Thanks to *Sundog Lit*, and then-editor Justin Daugherty, for publishing the short story that eventually turned into the prologue of this book.

My good friend Mike Ingram, one of the best readers and

editors I know, listened to me as I talked about this thing for years, and helped me solve some serious problems in the early drafts when I was ready to quit. This book was deeply influenced by a handful of books he made me read for our podcast, too, and so it surely wouldn't exist without him. Thank you to the Book Fight fans who have also had to listen to all this talk, but without the option of responding. Your support of the show is reaffirming on days when it seems like the only choice is to give up.

Thanks to the entire Barrelhouse team, my second family of talented, hilarious weirdos, who first gave me a home in the lit world and who help me to believe in the value of the writing community. Please consider this sentence a group hug that lasts a perfectly normal amount of time and then ends with us digging into some chicken from El Pollo Rico.

Lee Klein was the first classmate in grad school to treat me like I belonged there, and I've felt indebted to him ever since. His influence, as a reader, writer, and editor, is all over this book.

The First Year Writing Program at Temple has been a home for me for eleven years, and they've been incredibly supportive and flexible in helping me to get this work done.

I've been lucky to have many teachers over the years who have gone well beyond any reasonable expectation of a teacher, and I hope they all know how grateful I am for the ways they've encouraged me, guided me, demanded more of me, and just listened to me. Thanks especially to Dennis Bloh, Vince Kling, Justin Cronin, Geffrey Kelly, Brother Gerry Molyneaux, and Kevin Harty.

Above all, I owe thanks to my parents: Pat McAllister, who

believed in me long before I ever did; Joe McAllister, who taught me how to love books and who has missed out on all the fun parts; and Fred Long, my father-in-law, who told me, in the last conversation we would ever have, that he'd just finished my last book and he was proud to think of me as his son.

Comsewogue Public Library
170 Terryville Road
Port Jefferson Station, NY 11776